Jerome Cochran

The Yellow Fever Epidemic of 1873

The white blood-corpuscle

Jerome Cochran

The Yellow Fever Epidemic of 1873
The white blood-corpuscle

ISBN/EAN: 9783337390761

Printed in Europe, USA, Canada, Australia, Japan

Cover: Foto ©Andreas Hilbeck / pixelio.de

More available books at **www.hansebooks.com**

CONTRIBUTIONS TO THE TRANSACTIONS OF THE MEDICAL ASSO-
CIATION OF THE STATE OF ALABAMA—SESSION OF 1874

I.

THE YELLOW FEVER EPIDEMIC OF 1873.

II.

THE WHITE BLOOD-CORPUSCLE.

BY JEROME COCHRAN, M. D.,

*Professor of Public Hygiene and Medical Jurisprudence in the Medical College of
Alabama.*

MONTGOMERY, ALA.:

BARRETT & BROWN, BOOK AND JOB PRINTERS AND BINDERS.

1874.

THE YELLOW FEVER EPIDEMIC OF 1873.

BY JEROME COCHRAN, M. D.,

Professor of Public Hygiene and Medical Jurisprudence in the Medical College of Alabama.

CONTENTS:

PART FIRST.

THE HISTORY OF THE EPIDEMIC.

INTRODUCTORY.

In the arrangement of the various topics connected with the recent expidemic of yellow fever, I shall first give some account of the circumstances attending the advent and progress of the disease in the principal localities which it has invaded; and will then, in separate sections, discuss the more important questions involved in the consideration of its causes, its transportation from place to place, and the measures of prophylaxis employed against it.

I have taken much trouble to obtain full and accurate information. Nevertheless, it will be seen that in relation to most of the subjects mentioned, the detail of facts is inadequate and unsatisfactory. It is true, that many accounts of the epidemic have been published, especially of its behavior in those cities which have suffered from it most severely. But the more these accounts are studied, the more they are found to be superficial, uncritical, and unsatisfactory; and sometimes they are still worse—that is to say, they are equivocal, sophistical and false.

If the field of the inquiry afforded by the recent epidemic had been more industriously and more wisely cultivated, it is hardly to be doubted that valuable contributions would have been made to our knowledge of the natural history of yellow fever; and to the protective resources of public hygiene. But even as it is, the careful study of such facts as I have been able to collect will be found to yield us some items of important information.

I add here a tabular statement of the number of cases and the number of deaths which occurred in the several cities and towns which are included in my historical sketch. The number of cases has been obtained, in each instance, by rather loose methods of estimation, and nothing more can be claimed in the way of accuracy than a sort of general approximation towards the truth. The number of deaths, being obtained from actual records, may be accepted as substantially correct:

Yellow Fever in 1873—Cases and Deaths.

		Cases		Deaths
New Orleans—Cases		2,000	Deaths	226
Memphis,	"	10,000	"	2,000
Shreveport,	"	3,000	"	759
Pensacola,	"	600	"	61
Montgomery,	"	500	"	102
Calvert,	"	450	"	125
Mobile,	"	210	"	35
Totals—Cases		16,760	Deaths	3,308

If to these totals were added the cases and deaths in the

cities and towns and country places, which were visited with more or less severity by the epidemic, but which, for various reasons, I have been obliged to omit from my report, the number of cases would perhaps be swelled to a grand total of more than twenty thousand; while the aggregate of deaths would exceed three thousand five hundred. This would give an average mortality of 17½ *per centum* of the cases.

THE EPIDEMIC IN NEW ORLEANS.

The first case of yellow fever in New Orleans in 1873, which was also the first in the Mississippi Valley, occurred in the person of J. M. Arrua, mate of the Spanish bark Valparaiso. The Valparaiso left Havana on the 15th of June, in ballast, with twenty-one souls on board, all in good health. She arrived at the Mississippi quarantine station, below New Orleans, on the 24th of June, and was detained there for three full days, during which time she was thoroughly disinfected, twice with chlorine, and twice with carbolic acid. The disinfection was done both between decks and in the forecastle, and at night the hatches were left open for ventillation. She reached the city on the 26th or 27th of June, and was docked at pier 48, at the head of Second street, in the Fourth District, two miles above Canal street.

Arrua was taken sick with yellow fever on the 4th day of July, remained two days on the vessel, was then taken down to the Third District, a distance of three miles, to 448 Moreau street, where he died on the 8th of July. The vessel on which the attack commenced, and the house in which he died, were both subsequently disinfected. No other case of the disease occurred in either.

There is no question that this was a case of yellow fever, but there is some question as to where the disease was contracted. Was it in Havana? Or was it on board the Valparaiso? Or was it at the wharf in New Orleans? The Captain of the Valparaiso insists that Arrua contracted his sickness in New Orleans; and the New Orleans Board of Health admits that there are some grounds for this opinion.

Next above the Valparaiso, at the distance of about one hundred feet, lay the steamboat Belle Lee. The mate of this boat, Edward Hynes by name, was taken sick with yellow fever on the 12th of July, and died on board on the 20th. Subsequently, a carpenter and a painter, who had been employed on the Belle Lee, also sickened and died. In the meantime the boat was moved to the lower part of the Sixth District, and moored between Louisiana and Napoleon Avenues, at which point a new focus of infection was established, about which clustered thirty-seven cases and twenty-five deaths.

A little above the Belle Lee, the distance not mentioned, was the steamboat W. S. Pike. Three cases of yellow fever occurred on this boat—the first on the 28th of July, the second on the 29th, the third on the 30th.

During the months of August, September, and October, several other vessels were docked in this same neighborhood where the Valparaiso, the Lee and the Pike had become infected, and these also suffered severely, a considerable number of cases occurring on board of them, with several deaths. Several of these vessels were removed, like the Belle Lee, three miles below, to the Third District, and seem to have conveyed the infection to the wharves of that locality.

About half the cases occurring in the Third District originated on shipboard; and it is worthy of special remark that disinfection here utterly failed to check the progress of the disease. Dr. J. T. Newman, Sanitary Inspector of the District, tells us that "the forecastles and holds of infected ships were treated in the same manner as infected houses; but fresh cases occurred on the same ships even after the process of disinfection;" and it appears from other statements that cases continued to occur in this way in ships in which disinfection with carbolic acid had been several times repeated. This led to the suspicion that the wharves at which the vessels were anchored had become contaminated with the fever poison, and were the true sources of the infection. These structures were therefore subjected to the carbolic acid treatment; and after this was done we are told that the disease subsided. But was the subsidence due to the disinfection? This is what we are expected to believe, but it may be fairly doubted. The disinfection of the wharves was done on the 2d of November; but already a far more powerful agent of disinfection than carbolic acid had been at work. *There was frost on the 30th of October.*

In the Fourth District, according to the report of Dr. Alfred W. Perry, the Sanitary Inspector, there occurred altogether one hundred and twenty-three cases. The number that originated among the shipping is not stated. Neither do I find any account of the disinfection of vessels or of wharves in this district. If the vessels and wharves were disinfected it is a little surprising that the results of the experiment have not been reported. If they were not disinfected the health authorities, with their emphatic confidence in the efficacy of carbolic acid, are amenable to the charge of very strange and very culpable negligence. It was in this same Fourth District that the fever committed its principal ravages in 1871 and in 1872; but upon each occasion it has occupied a different portion of the district. In 1871 the region of greatest infection lay around the intersection of Washington and Magazine streets; in 1872, around the intersection of Jackson and Magazine streets; in 1873, between Chippewa street and the river. In July, of six cases in the district, all were between Chippewa street and the river. In August, of twenty-five cases, twenty-three were between Chippewa street and the river. In September, of fifty-four cases, forty-one were between Chippewa street and the river. In October, of thirty-two cases, eighteen were between Chippewa street and the river. In November, of six cases, three were between Chippewa street and the river. That is to say, in sums total, of one hundred and twenty-three cases in the district ninety-one were between Chippewa street and the river. General disinfection was commenced in this quarter of the city, as well as in other infected regions, during the first week in August. It was practiced without intermission, from week to week, and from month to month, on a more extensive scale than has ever been attempted anywhere else in the world. What was the result? Simply this: that the disease maintained the conflict on its chosen battlefield until the coming of the frost, unterrified and defiant to the last.

Up to the 13th day of November, one hundred and five cases of yellow fever were received into the Charity Hospital, an immense institution, which occupies an entire square, with a large number of internes, nurses, and patients sick of other diseases. Of these one hundred and five cases, twenty-seven had recovered, sixty-eight had died, and ten were still under treatment. No disinfection of any kind was practiced here; the disease manifested no disposition whatever to spread; and only two cases originated within the hospital.

Some general conception of the extent to which the aid of disinfection was invoked in New Orleans during this epidemic may be drawn from the fact that bills for disinfectants ordered by the President of the Board of Health were presented for payment to the Administrator of Police to the aggregate amount of sixteen thousand two hundred and seventy-one dollars, ($16,271.)

The total number of cases reported to the Board of Health for the year is three hundred and eighty-eight. The total number of deaths is two hundred and twenty-six. This represents a mortality of 58.24 per centum, and would indicate a type of disease of almost unprecedented and altogether appalling malignity. But the figures representing the number of cases, notwithstanding their official character, are entirely unreliable. Indeed, it is safe to say that they do not make even a distant approximation towards the truth. It is known that physicians generally made it a rule not to report to the Board of Health the cases they had under treatment. As Dr. Tebault expresses it, they forbore to make the diagnosis, and only reported, in order to escape fines, such cases as threatened a fatal termination. The real aggregate of cases must have approached two thousand, or about five times the number reported by the Board of Health.

During the yellow fever season there was a damp atmosphere, and a great deal of rain. The thermometric means range from 79° to 88° Fahrenheit.

Concurrently with the epidemic of yellow fever there was a very general and widespread epidemic of dengue in New Orleans. The New Orleans *Medical and Surgical Journal* estimates the number of cases at fifty thousand. The Board of Health estimate that one-half of the entire population of the city were afflicted by it, which would swell the number to about one hundred thousand cases. Six deaths are ascribed to it as being caused by the exhaustion consequent on protracted attacks.

The account which I have given of the epidemic in New Orleans is derived chiefly from the report of the Board of Health, and from the article of Dr. Tebault in the February number of the Richmond and Louisville *Medical Journal*.

THE EPIDEMIC IN MEMPHIS.

Yellow Fever was brought to Memphis in 1873 by the steam towboat Bee, which ran between New Orleans and St. Louis. She had been with her barges in New Orleans at the infected wharf of the Fourth District, in the same neighborhood with the Valparaiso and the Belle Lee. Three or four of her crew, including the captain, were taken sick with the fever during her trip up the river. She reached Memphis on the 10th of August, and remained there several hours. Two sick deck passengers were put ashore at the foot of Market street, in the neighborhood afterwards so famous in the annals of the epidemic as Happy Hollow. One of these, whose name is not known, staggered into a shanty near the wharf, occupied by an Irishman named Riley, and died there the next day. The name of the other man was W. W. Davis, who lived in Lauderdale county, Alabama. He passed the night in the Adams Street station-house, where he died the next morning. There were two deaths, therefore, on the 11th. The captain, C. B. Goll, remained on the boat and died the next night at Osceola, Arkansas, ninety miles above Memphis. His body was brought back to Memphis and shipped by express to St. Louis. The infection did not spread from either Mr. Davis or Captain Goll, but proceeded first to make the conquest of Happy Hollow. It has been made a question, and it is one of considerable importance, whether the true source of the infection was the unknown unfortunate who died in Riley's cabin, or whether the germs of the pestilence emanated from the boat itself. It is to be regretted for many reasons, that the future history of the boat was not ascertained. Here, at any rate, at the foot of Market street, where was located Riley's cabin and the wharf at which the boat had landed, the epidemic first declared its malignant presence.

The first victim claimed from the population of the city, was a young man, name not given, who had rendered some humane assistance to the poor stranger who died at Riley's. Riley himself was then stricken down and soon died, but the date of his death is not given. As nearly always happens in the beginning of epidemics, the true nature of these first cases was not appreciated; and so unrecognized and utterly careless of recognition the dreadful malady began its work of desolation. Its progress at first was slow, but it never faltered in its march.

During some weeks its depredations were confined to Happy Hollow. "What in Memphis is called Happy Hollow is a very low, flat, area of about four acres, immediately on the river, near the northern limit of the city. It is under the Chickasaw Bluffs, so sunken that during high water it is largely submerged; but after the river has fallen it is left partially covered with stagnant ponds and slimy ooze, whose exhalations are noisome and offensive. Its soil is alluvial, and upon this garbage has been continuously thrown until it has become extremely filthy. It is the natural drain for the gutters of the over-hanging bluffs, through which sewerage steadily trickles. It is in addition, the home of a low class of Irish, and the favorite landing place of flats and rafts, whose occupants are proverbial for their carelessness and uncleanliness. During the hot summer months this accumulated mass of filth lies festering and rotting in the sun, exhaling mephitic gasses, and only needing the germs of yellow fever to be sown upon it to yield the fearful fruits of a great epidemic."—(*Dr. Erskine.*) I have no information of the number of persons inhabiting this locality; nor of the number of deaths occurring among them; nor of the rate of mortality.

By the first of September the disease had reached the top of the bluff, a distance of some three hundred yards from the point of departure. The height of the bluff is not stated in the accounts which I have read, but it must be something like one hundred feet. Having overleaped this barrier, the disease continued its onward march, moving slowly from house to house, and from square to square, until it occupied the northern third of the city.

It was declared epidemic on the 14th of September. Soon after this it set all boundaries at defiance and swept over the whole city. The wind seems to have had but little to do with its dissemination. It is described as having been fearfully infectious.

The temperature ranged from 75° to 85° Fahrenheit. There were several heavy rains during the prevalence of the epidemic, which had no perceptible effect upon the fever, certainly no favorable effect.

No measures of isolation were attempted. It is worthy of remark, however, that the jail, which was in the heart of the district which suffered most severely, escaped invasion until the 8th or 10th of October, when one of the prisoners, Fred Brooks by name, was attacked. He was removed to the Walthall Infirmary, where he died. Another case occurred shortly afterwards, which was treated in the jail and recovered. There were quite a number of cases of sickness in the jail which were regarded as dengue, all of whom recovered. The average number of prisoners was about one hundred and twenty-five. The sanitary condition of the institution received very careful attention. It was fumigated twice a day by burning coal tar; carbolic acid was freely used as a disinfectant; and it was thoroughly washed from top to bottom once or twice a week by means of water pipes laid for the purpose. It was surrounded by a wall fifteen feet high ; and intercourse with the outside world was restrained within very narrow limits. It is to the high wall and non-intercourse that Dr. Erskine, who had charge of it, attributes its comparative exemption. ·

As soon as the epidemic was fully established, spasmodic efforts began to be made in the way of disinfection. But at this time there was no Board of Health, and everything was done without system and without intelligent direction. A Board of Health was finally organized on the 8th of October, after the fever had been raging for two months. Of this Board Dr. Erskine was President, and under his administration very energetic efforts were made to check the further progress of the pestilence. Carbolic acid was used in large quantities, and lime was scattered freely in the yards and gutters ; but without any perceptible influence, either good or bad.

There was some dengue at first, and some malarial fever ; but these milder maladies were soon swept away, and the more malignant disease took possession of the field, as is always the case in great epidemics. Dr. LeMonnier, in the New Orleans Medical Journal, undertakes to prove that the fever was of a mixed type—a hybrid monster, part yellow fever and part malarial fever. He is undoubtedly mistaken. First, because no such mixture of febrile types has ever been known to occur, or by possibility could occur. And secondly, because there is no such general prevalence of malarial fevers in Memphis as would be necessary to furnish the malarial part of the parentage in this unnatural conjugation.· And thirdly, because the proof is overwhelming that the disease was unmitigated and unmistakable malignant yellow fever—yellow fever pure and simple, without admixture with anything else.

The first frost was on the 5th of November. New cases of the disease, with the usual percentage of deaths, continued to occur until the middle of December. Some of these, I am unable to state how many, were among returned refugees. This unusual persistence of the pestilence after there had been several times severe frost and ice, is one of the remarkable features of its history.

The population of Memphis at the advent of the epidemic may be stated at about 45,000. In the general exodus that ensued it is estimated that 20,000 persons sought safety in flight, leaving 25,000 at the mercy of the pestilence. The number of cases is roughly estimated at from 7,000 to 10,000. The mortality is stated by Dr. Eskine at 1,800. But I have seen a list of the deaths containing 2,000 names. Upon this basis the mortality is from 20 to 25 *per centum* of the cases.

There are some circumstances connected with this Memphis epidemic, not of a medical character, which are worthy of mention even in this brief account of it.

When the stricken city found herself in the dreadful embrace of the pestilence, she was obliged to send abroad an appeal for help. To this appeal the whole country, from Maine to California, and from the rice fields and palmetto groves of South Carolina to the pine forests and frozen lakes of the North-west, responded in most liberal contributions of money and supplies. The subjoined table will show the amounts received by the various Associations which were engaged in the relief of the sick, and also the amounts left on hand at the close of the pestilence:

ASSOCIATIONS,	RECEIVED.	REMAINING.
Howard Association	$124,245	$46,919
Masonic Relief	32,926	16,699
Odd Fellows' Relief	46,606	30,982
German Relief	8,576	1,108
Citizens' Relief	91,713	11,506
Fire Relief	5,548	3,121
Shoulder to Shoulder	2,501	141
Police Relief	12,875	7,426
Knights of Pythias	6,579	1,949
Totals	$331,589	$119,848

From this it will be seen that large as was the demand for assistance, the contributions made were still larger, showing an aggregate net excess of 120,000 dollars—more than one-third of the aggregate sum of the contributions.

For information respecting the epidemic in Memphis, I have relied almost entirely on the published reports of Dr. Erskine, who was President of the Memphis Board of Health, and upon private letters which he has been kind enough to write in reply to my inquiries.

THE EPIDEMIC IN SHREVEPORT.

For the facts in connection with the Epidemic in Shreveport in 1873 I am obliged to depend entirely on two reports: 1st, the Report of Drs. A. B. Snell, D. P. Fenner, and J. F. Davis, made to the Shreveport Medical Society and published by the Howard Association; 2d, the Report of Dr. Henry Smith to the Louisiana Equitable Life Insurance Company of New Orleans.

These reports are both extremely defective in all that relates to the introduction of the disease into the City of Shreveport. According to Dr. Smith, it broke out almost simultaneously in three separate localities, namely: on Texas street in the center of the city near where the Transatlantic Circus was quartered; in a Levee street boarding house; and at a point near the river two miles below the city; but the dates of its appearance in these several localities are not given. A little further on he states that the first case, which he considers as a doubtful one, although it terminated in death, occurred on the 18th of August; and that a second case, certainly genuine yellow fever, occurred on the 22d of August. The result of this last case is not given; and I can only conjecture that this also terminated fatally; and that the dates given mark the periods of the death of, and not the beginnings of, the cases.

The Report of the Committee of the Shreveport Medical Society states that the first case occurred in the person of Newton Walker. It is not quite certain that his case was really one of yellow fever, but the circumstantial evidence that it was so is nearly conclusive. He was engaged in his store, on the Levee at the corner of Crockett street, every day in settling up his business affairs, and took his meals at an eating house which was patronized by steamboatmen. He took sick on the 12th of August, and went to the house of his brother near Bayou Pierre, three miles below the city. He was not seen by a physician during the febrile stage of his malady, but was subsequently treated for "yellow jaundice." The real nature of his attack was not suspected until several members of his brother's family were taken sick with yellow fever, of which five of them died. There was no way to trace the infection in these cases except through Newton Walker. It is not stated whether the fever was propagated from this stricken family to other families in the neighborhood. And it is to be specially remarked that while Newton Walker is supposed to have contracted the disease inside of the city, he passed through its various stages three miles below the city. It is also to be specially remarked that there is no intimation in either of these reports that the epidemic within the city limits proper was derived in any way from this suburban outbreak.

I suppose that this is the first of the three localities mentioned by Dr. Smith, although the distance below the city is stated by him at two miles instead of three. It was in this neighborhood that a steamboat had sunk with a considerable number of cattle on board, which were drowned. They were afterwards dragged ashore and skinned, and their carcasses left to rot in the open air.

By the 25th of August, we are told, the number of cases had so greatly increased that the physicians found themselves overwhelmed with calls. We are also told that the disease was at this time mostly confined to public boarding houses which were frequented by river men. The fever now spread in the central portion of the city with great rapidity, and was epidemic on the first of September. The number of cases and of deaths continued to increase from day to day until the middle of September, by which time the pestilence had swept over the whole city. After this there was little variation in the death rate until the 20th of October, when there was a mild frost. A few days later, namely, on the 28th and

29th, there was heavy frost and ice, and the grasp of the enemy was felt at once to relax.

At the first alarm a large number of the inhabitants left; and many others a little later, seeing the dreadful mortality of the pestilence, fled panic-stricken. Of these a considerable proportion went away with the germs of the malady in their systems, and were stricken down in their several places of refuge. It is said that more than half the cases attacked in this way died; and that in many instances they spread the infection to persons about them, so as in some cases to develop destructive epidemics—as for example in Calvert and in Marshall.

The population of Shreveport was about ten thousand. It is estimated that more than half of these left during the exodus which has been described, so that only about four thousand five hundred persons, black and white, remained in the city. The number of cases is estimated at three thousand. The number of deaths was seven hundred and fifty-nine. The blacks were attacked almost as generally as the whites, but the mortality amongst them was very much less— six hundred and thirty-nine whites dying, and one hundred and twenty blacks; the color of the remaining cases not being mentioned. The ratio of deaths to cases was about twenty-five *per centum.*

The type of the fever was intensely malignant and infectious. The average period of incubation seemed to be about seven days; but in some it was as short as three days, and in some as long as three weeks.

The scanty detail of facts, as I have given them, leaves the origin of the epidemic enveloped in some doubt. Much stress has been laid on the filthy and unsanitary condition of the city on account of defective drainage and neglect of scavengering. But this unsanitary condition of the city has existed for many years which have not been marked with epidemics. Besides, while defective drainage and filth may render yellow fever more malignant, it is well known that they will not of themselves produce it. It was very widely asserted at the beginning of the epidemic, that it had been brought by a traveling circus company from Mexico across the State of Texas. But it was shown afterwards that the circus people contracted the disease at Shreveport, instead of bringing it with them. Another favorite theory was, that it was caused by the removal of the famous Red River raft; but the following statement is a sufficient refutation of this theory: It is a fact, that from fifty to one hundred men were constantly employed during the season in clearing out the raft, and that not a single case of yellow fever occurred amongst them.

From the fact that the first cases all seem to have occurred among persons who were in the habit of associating with steamboat and river men, and that even after the disease had made considerable progress, it was still mostly confined to boarding houses frequented by steamboat men and river men, I think it is perfectly legitimate to conclude, that the infection was brought in some way up the river from New Orleans.

The only notable peculiarity of the season meteorologically is, that it was more than usually damp—the air more than usually humid.

THE EPIDEMIC IN PENSACOLA.

The yellow fever in Pensacola, in 1873, seems to be clearly traceable to the ship Golden Dream. This vessel reached the harbor of Pensacola on the 10th of June. She had lost three of her crew at Havana, and eight more while at sea. She was therefore placed in quarantine, cleaned, fumigated, and whitewashed, and detained for twenty-four days before she was allowed to approach the city. She was anchored about five hundred yards from the central wharf. This brings us to the 3d of July. A month elapsed without any event of importance, when a sailor who had been eight days on board the Golden Dream was taken sick with the fever on the 2d day of August. He died with black vomit on the 5th. The Golden Dream sailed on the 16th of August, and was lost at sea on the 30th, in consequence, it is said, of "getting short of hands," her crew having been stricken down by the pestilence.

The first three cases that occurred within the city were all attacked on the same day, namely, the 6th of August, and in the same house, the residence of Mr. W. McKinzie Orthing, Deputy Harbor Master, on Romana street, two squares distant from the water's edge. On the next day, the 7th, four other cases occurred on Romana street, near Mr. Orthing's house. The first death in the city was that of Mrs. Nasite, who arrived in Pensacola from New Orleans on the 22d of July, was taken sick two weeks after, namely, on the 7th of August, and died on the 13th. Between the 7th and the 14th several stevedores who had been employed on the infected vessel contracted the fever, and communicated it to their families, thus establishing almost at the same time several different centers of infection.

It will have been remarked that the first eight or ten cases in the city had no direct communication with the Golden Dream. How, then, did they become infected? Mr. Orthing had visited the vessel repeatedly, but, while the inmates of his house were stricken down, he himself escaped. He might have brought the poison with him in his clothing, even as Dr. McDonald, the author of the article on Yellow Fever in Reynolds' Practice, tells us that he often trembled to think that his monkey jacket might become a vehicle of infection. But the more probable opinion seems to be, that it was in the wings of the invisible swift winds that the seeds of the pestilence found agents of transportation. We are told that the wind, from the 28th of July until after the fever became epidemic, blew steadily every day, between the hours of five and ten P. M., from the south-west, sweeping first over the infected ship, and then over that portion of the city in which these cases made their appearance, the distance to be traversed being about half a mile. We are also told that the disease spread rapidly for more than a mile towards the north-east, the direction traveled by the wind, along a narrow belt about one square in width; and that it was confined almost exclusively to this belt for some ten days. Afterwards it spread all over the city.

The atmosphere was damp and humid, even in the absence of clouds. There were but three entirely fair days in June, ten in July, and twelve in August. The rain was abundant, and fell in torrents. The mean temperature for June was 78° Fah., for July 80°, for August 81°. Electricity negative: ozone altogether absent.

The population was reduced by stampede to about three thousand, of whom about one thousand were liable to the disease. The number of cases is estimated at six hundred. The number of deaths was sixty-one—ten *per centum*. As usual, the whites suffered most severely; but the blacks were not entirely exempt. There was no dengue. Disinfection, as a means of prophylaxis, was not attempted. I am indebted to Dr. Hargis, of Pensacola, for most of the facts given in this sketch.

THE EPIDEMIC IN MONTGOMERY.

After an interval of exemption of eighteen years, Montgomery was called to suffer from another visitation of yellow fever in 1873. It is believed that the disease was brought from Pensacola by a white woman named Mollie Jackson, and by Mr. D. H. Cram, President of the Pensacola and Louisville Railroad.

Mollie Jackson had been living in Pensacola opposite the hospital. It has been stated in the account of the epidemic in Pensacola, that yellow fever had made its appearance there in three cases on the 6th of August, and in four cases on the 7th, and that it had traveled in the direction of the wind with extraordinary rapidity. Mollie Jackson left Pensacola on the 9th, and had therefore been sufficiently exposed to the infectious influence. She arrived in Montgomery on the 10th, sickened on the 17th, and died on the 26th. During the first four days of her illness, she was seen by a physician who did not suspect that he had a case of yellow fever. The fever subsided, and the physician saw her no more; but notwithstanding her apparent recovery, she relapsed in a few days and died. The extreme yellowness of the dead body, together with information derived from the nurses, afterwards satisfied the physician in question that it was really a case of specific yellow fever. One of the nurses went to West Point, Georgia, was very ill with fever, and is stated to have thrown up blood from the stomach.

From the house, situated near the intersection of Clay and Dickerson streets, in the First Ward, in which Mollie Jackson died, as a focus of infection, the fever spread through the surrounding neighborhood. Almost every house in the three adjoining blocks was invaded, and death after death by black vomit proclaimed the character of the malady.

Mr. Cram's residence was at the corner of McDonough and Madison streets, in the Fifth Ward. He left Pensacola on the 14th day of August and reached Montgomery on the 15th. His office in Pensacola was in the infected region. He got sick somewhere between the 17th and the 20th with a fever which lasted several days. Its character does not seem to have been accurately determined; but on account of his Pensacola exposure, and of subsequent events in his neighborhood it is presumed to have been yellow fever. Here at any rate was in some way established a new focus of infection The husband of Mr. Cram's nurse died soon after in the same yard of yellow fever—date of death not given. On the 4th of September the house next to Mr. Cram's on Madison street, which was occupied by Germans, was invaded, and up to the 25th five deaths had occurred in it. Next to Mr. Cram's on McDonough street, is a row of brick buildings, not one of which escaped.

For some two or three weeks the disease was confined to the two neighborhoods that have been mentioned; but ultimately it extended all over the city. The white population. fled in dismay until not more than eighteen hundred remained in the stricken city. Of these it is believed that nearly five hundred had the fever. A considerable number of negroes were also attacked, enough probably to swell the aggregate of cases to full five hundred or more. There were one hundred and two deaths—eighty reported by the Board of Health and twenty-two derived from other sources of information. The mortality, therefore, was about twenty *per centum* of the cases.

The disease was of a milder type among the negroes than among the whites, and very few of them died. Twelve deaths are accredited to Ward One, and sixty to Ward Five; leaving thirty scattered over the rest of the city.

Before the arrival of the fever some measures of disinfection had been practiced with a view to the prevention of cholera, such as the use of lime in gutters and foul places, and the use of carbolic acid in the vaults of privies, and the city was considered to be in a good sanitary condition. While the fever was in progress large quantities of coal tar were burnt in the streets, but the fumes evolved exhibited no power to check the march of the pestilence.

I have obtained the information which I have detailed in this account of the Epidemic in Montgomery chiefly from the Report of Dr. R. F. Michel, which was published in the January number of the Charleston Medical Journal.

THE EPIDEMIC IN CALVERT.

On the 3d of September, a young man by the name of Hughes arrived in Calvert fleeing from yellow fever in Shreveport. He had been in business there as a clerk, and the fever had been prevailing for some time before he left. He was taken sick at the Haynes House on the night of the 5th of September, presented all the symptoms of malignant yellow fever, and died on the 10th. On the night of the 10th the clerk of the Haynes House, who had waited on Hughes, began to complain and had a mild attack of fever, from which he recovered in a few days. But subsequently he relapsed and died of black vomit—date of death not stated. The disease now begun to spread through the village. Mrs. Haynes, the proprietor of the hotel, was taken sick on the 23d and died with black vomit on the 27th. Dr. Coleman, who had treated the cases at the Haynes House, was attacked on the 28th. He recovered, but the disease spread through his family to the extent of six cases.

The bedding on which Hughes died was thrown upon the roof of a little house at the foot of Main street, and left there exposed to wind and weather for three weeks, the prevailing wind in the meantime blowing almost directly up the street and scattering the poison over the town. By the 20th of October the pestilence became general.

The town contained a white population of about fifteen hundred. Only a little over six hundred of these remained during the prevalence of the fever, and among this devoted six hundred there occurred at least four hundred and fifty cases and one hundred and twenty-five deaths—a mortality of about twenty-eight *per centum.*

It is stated that an unusually large number of relapses occurred here, some as long as six weeks after the first attack, and many of them fatal. A considerable number of pregnant females had the fever, but not one of them miscarried or died. It was remarked, that the pulse during convalescence, and even weeks after the recovery, was greatly increased in rapidity—varying from ninety to a hundred and twenty per minute.

The first frost was near the end of October. It seemed to have no effect whatever on the progress of the epidemic. The material was indeed nearly consumed, but fifteen cases subsequently occurred, eight of them among returned refugees and new comers. There were several frosts in November, but these also seemed not to lessen the virulence of the infection. The last case, a returned refugee, was taken sick on the 20th of December, and died on the 29th.

From Calvert the disease was transported to several places in the adjacent country. In at least three of these it spread to the extent of three or four cases in each place—most of them fatal. A gentleman and his family fleeing from the infected town, passed the first night with a relative at Owensville, twelve miles distant. They went on the next day, borrowing a blanket and a shawl for one of their children which had fallen sick. One day later these articles were returned. Within a few days three cases of yellow fever occurred in the family, and two of them died with black vomit. They had no other communication with any infected place.

No disinfection was attempted in Calvert until the 1st of December, when the houses that had been closed were opened for ventillation, and carbolic acid scattered in the rooms with a view to the destruction of the lurking germs of the pestilence.

This account has been condensed from that given by Dr. Coleman in the March number of the New Orleans Medical Journal.

THE EPIDEMIC AT GREENWOOD.

The principal interest of the little outbreak of yellow fever in the neighborhood of Greenwood is in connection with its occurrence in the family of Dr. F., a wealthy planter living four miles east of the town. This family consisted of Dr. F., aged 76 years; Captain F., his son, aged 48 years; nine children of Captain F., aged from 8 to 25 years; and several colored servants. Two of the sons had been employed in Shreveport, where the fever was at the time epidemic. These two young men, Harris and Voss, aged respectively 22 years and 19 years, came home on the 28th of September, seemingly in good health, and without baggage. The next day Harris was taken sick; and on the day following Voss also sickened. Voss recovered in two days, the nature of his sickness not having been determined; but Harris had all the symptoms of yellow fever, and died on the 3rd of October with black vomit and suppression of urine. The mattress on which he had lain was exposed to the air for some thirty-six hours, during which time a slight shower of rain fell upon it. It was returned to the room about the 5th, and used as a bed by other members of the family. The blankets and sheets were washed by a colored servant and replaced on the same bed. The servant fell sick in a day or two after the washing, and died on the 11th. She had not been about Harris during his illness, and could have contracted the disease only from the clothing which she had washed. The room in which

Harris died was used during the day by all the family, and at night by Voss and Robert as a bed-room. On the 9th or 10th sickness again appeared in the household ; and on the 13th Dr. G. N. Riggins was called in. He found four cases of yellow fever, namely : Robert, aged 25 years, Voss, aged 19, Lucien, aged 13, and Kelso, aged 10. They were all mild attacks except one. Robert had black vomit, but recovered.

On the 15th Dr. F., the grandfather, was taken sick with the fever. He slept in a detached building distant about twenty feet from his son's house ; but he had been with his grandsons during their sickness, and had allowed one of the sick children to share his bed. He died on the 29th of the month.

About the 10th of October, Captain F. returned home after an absence of five days, during which he had received a gunshot wound of the shoulder which confined him to his bed. He slept in a room at the opposite side of the hall from the room in which Harris had died. The hall was ten feet wide. Some of the children suffering from yellow fever occupied a bed in the same room with the Captain. He took the disease on the 19th and died of it on the 23rd.

In addition to these cases a colored boy who had waited on Dr. F., and who had washed some clothing on which urine and fœces had been passed, was taken ill with the fever about the 20th. He recovered. Four of the children escaped infection, as did also the neighbors who visited the family during their affliction. There was no local cause to account for the sickness.

Nine other cases occurred in and around the town in the persons of refugees from Shreveport; but no infection either of persons or of localities resulted from any of these. Free ventilation was the only prophylactic measure employed.

These details are gathered from a communication to the New Orleans Medical Journal by Dr. M. F. Leary, U. S. A., Post Surgeon at Greenwood.

THE EPIDEMIC IN MOBILE.

The first case of yellow fever in Mobile in 1873 was that of Owen McKenna. He was employed in the workshops of the Mobile and New Orleans Railroad; went to New Orleans on the 16th of August; returned to Mobile on the 17th; was taken sick on the 21st; and died with black vomit on the 26th, at the house of Mr. Casey, on the east side of Hamilton street, between Palmetto and Charleston. An interval of five weeks elapsed before any other cases occurred in this vicinity. On the 6th of October, Dr. F. M. Stone died near the corner of Franklin and Charleston, one block east of Mr. Casey's; and subsequently a few additional cases occurred in this section of the city, but at a distance of several squares. I am not able to say whether the infection in these cases was derived from Owen McKenna, or from some other source.

The second case in the city was that of Edward Dixon. This man had been employed in the neighborhood of Shreveport, and spent some hours in that city on his way to Mobile. He passed through New Orleans without detention, and arrived in Mobile on the 10th of September. He was already sick, but went that same evening across the bay. He returned to the city the next morning, September 11th. He was now very sick, and was found under an old shed near the wharf by Policeman Dougherty, who, by direction of the City Physician, took him to the City Hospital, where he died on the 13th of unmistakable and malignant yellow fever. It was from this case that the epidemic was engendered. In order that its dissemination may be easily understood it is necessary to premise a few topographical details.

The City Hospital, the focus of infection, is just one mile from the river in the north-west quarter of the city. The streets here that are parallel with the river run very nearly from north-west to south-east. Of this range of streets we shall have occasion to mention Wilkerson, Jefferson, and Broad, the last being the most remote from the river of the three. Other streets cross these at right angles, running from the river to Broad street and beyond, and consequently pursuing a direction nearly from north-east to south-west. Of these we shall have occasion to mention St. Antony, Congress, and Adams. The City Hospital lies between Broad and Jefferson, on the north-east side of St. Antony. To the north-east of the City Hospital and separated from it by a high brick wall is the jail, which also lies between Broad and Jefferson, fronting on Congress. In the same range, south-west of the City Hospital, on the opposite side of St. Antony street, is Providence Infirmary. On the same side of St. Antony street as the City Hospital, separated from it by Jefferson street, and so lying one square nearer to the river, is the Marine Hospital. Each of these institutions occupies an entire square. Across Broad street, just beyond the City Hospital and the jail, are several squares that are very nearly vacant. Sweeping past the south-west corner of Providence Infirmary, in a direction a little north of west, is the Spring Hill Road. A few hundred feet further towards the south, and very nearly parallel with the Spring Hill Road, is the Spring Hill Shell Road. To reach the Spring Hill Road from the City Hospital by the shortest route it is necessary to cross one square in a diagonal direction. To reach the Shell Road two squares must be crossed diagonally. Passing down Broad street towards the south-east, we come, at the distance of eight squares, to Canal street. Here Broad street changes its direction, and runs almost directly to the south, bearing however slightly to the west. The next street after crossing Canal is Palmetto—which is thus nine squares from the City Hospital. Next west of Broad in this part of its course, and parallel with it, is Marine street.

The infection confined itself chiefly to a narrow belt extending from north to south, almost along Broad street, with the City Hospital near its northern extremity, and Palmetto street near its southern boundary. Along this belt there were established three special yellow fever centres—the first at the City Hospital; the second beyond Broad street, on the Spring

Hill Road and the Shell Road, the third also beyond Broad, and about the intersection of Palmetto and Marine.

As we have already seen, the disease was carried to the City Hospital by Edward Dixon, who died there on the 13th of September. Nine other cases occurred in the Hospital, making ten in all, with five deaths. One of these was Sister Xavier.

The second case in this neighborhood was that of Sister Regina, who was taken sick on the 15th of September, and died on the 18th, in the Providence Infirmary. Altogether four cases originated in this Infirmary, with three deaths. Seven cases are reported as having occurred in the Marine Hospital, with one death. In the immediate neighborhood there occurred several additional cases, with several deaths—exact number not ascertained. Throughout this neighborhood carbolic acid was abundantly used as a prophylactic, commencing with the earliest cases; but it most signally failed, either to check the progress of the malady, or to modify its type.

Passing along the infected belt towards the north-west, we find that the jail escaped infection altogether. Not a single decided case occurred within its walls during the season. There was one doubtful case in the person of the Jailor, Mr. J. E. Collins, who had a mild attack of some sort of fever, commencing November 2d. It is stated that this institution has always enjoyed a similar immunity during all previous epidemics. It is surrounded by a high brick wall, and necessarily has but little communication with the rest of the city. There were a few cases still further north than the jail, but they require no special mention.

In the infected neighborhood lying beyond Broad street and along the Spring Hill Road and the Shell Road, a few hundred yards South of the City Hospital, there occurred a larger number of cases than in any other part of the city. Here, on the Spring Hill Road, cases occurred as early as the 23d of September, and on the Shell Road as early as the 25th, the epidemic traveling slowly south and west. Amongst other cases in this neighborhood were those of Policeman Dougherty and his son. Dougherty, it will be remembered, was the policeman who assisted Edward Dixon to the hospital. Carbolic acid was freely and repeatedly used in this neighborhood also, but, as in the case of the hospital and its vicinity, it failed utterly, either to check the progress of the malady, or to modify its type. The fever pursued the even tenor of its way until a mightier disinfectant than carbolic acid lent its aid, namely, frost. And even after frost several cases, and several deaths among returned refugees whose residences were in this part of the city, showed that the poison still lingered in its chosen haunts.

Taking now a great leap to the south, and passing over some six squares with only an occasional case to mark its transit, the disease made its appearance on the 1st of October on Palmetto street, near Marine, the third of the infected neighborhoods which I have indicated in this belt. The first case here was John McCann, who sickened on the 28th of September, and died on the 1st day of October. He is said to have been much about the City Hospital, where he may have contracted the disease. On the 17th and 18th of October, four other members of the McCann family were stricken down— father, mother, and two children. The mother and one child died, both on the 21st. Eight or ten additional cases occurred in this immediate neighborhood, with several additional deaths. Here again carbolic acid disinfection was used with lavish profusion, and here also it proved to be utterly destitute of prophylactic virtue.

Ten cases, with five deaths, occurred outside of the city limits, in the western suburbs about three miles from the river, in the neighborhood of Smith's dumping ground—a place of most unfragrant reputation, where dead animals and the contents of privy vaults are transformed into commercial fertilizers. The atmosphere of this place is said to have been very offensive at the time; and whether from this cause or some other, the cases occurring here were exceedingly malignant, as the rate of mortality, 50 *per centum*, sufficiently shows.

People living in this neighborhood were obliged to pass through the Broad street belt to get to the city, and it is probable that these cases originated in this way. Or it may be that the excretions of yellow fever patients were conveyed in privy filth to the dumping ground. Mrs. Smith was the first victim.

As far as I have been able to learn, there was but one case among our negro population—the case, namely, of Maria Wheeler, who died on the 17th of November.

In compiling the statistics of epidemics, it is always impossible to ascertain exactly either the number of cases or of deaths. But I have taken much trouble to get at the truth as nearly as possible in regard to both of these points in our recent visitation of yellow fever; and I am satisfied that my information is far more accurate than is usually obtained in such cases. I have been able to collect reports of two hundred cases and thirty deaths occurring in the city; and of ten cases and five deaths occurring in the suburbs. The ratio of mortality to cases in the city is, therefore, fifteen *per centum.*

I have reports of fifty-two cases occurring in forty-six houses which were not disinfected, so that in forty separate houses where there was no disinfection no second case presented itself—a most effective reply to the argument that because carbolic acid may have been used in a house without the occurrence of a second case, that therefore the subsequent exemption was due to the carbolic acid.

Of the two hundred cases reported, the source of infection was traced in one hundred and thirty, and always, directly or indirectly to Edward Dixon. Twelve cases, with three or four deaths among them, are reported as occurring after frost.

I append a meteorological table for the year. It presents nothing specially remarkable. We had heavy rains in August, and local thunder storms almost every day, with an aggregate of sixteen inches of rain. Maximum thermometer 94°, minimum 70°, mean 80°.26'; prevailing wind, south. In September rains and thunderstorms continued to be frequent, rain sixteen inches. Maximum thermometer 91°, minimum 61°, mean 76°.16'; prevailing wind from the north-east. In October, rain five inches; maximum thermometer 87°, minimum 34°, mean 65°.22'; prevailing wind from the north; first noticeable frost on the 26th.

Along with our epidemic of yellow fever we had a much more extensive epidemic of dengue. I am not able to make even an approximate estimate of the number of cases; there were no deaths.

In consequence of the epidemic there was complete prostration of business, and from eight thousand to ten thousand of our people went away to escape the infection. The excitement was out of all proportion to the danger. All of the most populous parts of the city escaped with comparative impunity. Inside of the infected neighborhoods there was indeed considerable danger; but outside of the infected neighborhoods the danger was very slight. I sincerely believe that our commerce ought not to have suffered interruption; and that strangers could have visited with perfect safety, and at any time during the season, any of the business parts of the city. Because yellow fever prevailed about the City Hospital, and in a narrow belt beyond Broad street, a mile or more from the river, it does not follow that pestilence was lying in ambush among the dry goods and grocery houses of Water and Commerce streets, and the hotels and restaurants of Royal. A few strangers did venture into the city during the reign of the epidemic, and I have not learned that any of them suffered on account of their temerity.

A quasi quarantine was established against the West Indies, New Orleans, and Pensacola. But it was not put into operation until the disease which it was intended to exclude had already entered the city. It was moreover of such imperfect character that it was easily evaded, and in point of fact was evaded repeatedly. It is therefore unnecessary for any purpose I have in view to give any detailed account of it. If, however, I were writing a history of municipal folly it would be worthy of special mention.

The account which I have given of this epidemic of yellow

fever in Mobile has been prepared partly from my own knowledge of the facts, and partly from information furnished me by several of our leading physicians in written reports of their own practice. I am aware that it differs very widely from the report of our Advisory Board of Health ; but not for that reason is it any the less worthy of confidence. Doubtless the Board of Health did the best they could under the circumstances; but circumstances were singularly unfavorable to them, inasmuch as most of our physicians persistently refused to report to them, or to recognize them in any other light than as public nuisances.

THE REPORT OF THE ADVISORY BOARD OF HEALTH.

But it is necessary that I should be a little more exp'icit concerning the report of the Advisory Board of Health, or rather, the report of the Medical Officer of that Board.

This report bears date the 1st day of November, 1873, and was published under the auspices of the Board in the Daily Register, newspaper, of the 27th of the same month. The material portions of it had been communicated to the American Public Health Association, at its session in New York, on the 12th of November, and is to be published in the Transactions of that body. It is, moreover, the only official account of our late epidemic which has been given to the world, and will naturally be made use of by medical historians and statisticians. In the interests of historical and scientific accuracy, therefore, it becomes important that its mistakes should be corrected and its deficiencies supplied.

I quote *verbatim* the summary of cases and deaths :

"The total number of cases treated in the city, as officially reported, is as follows : Sixteen cases occurred in the hospitals, of which number seven died and nine recovered. Outside of the hospitals there were twenty-two cases, of which number twelve died and ten recovered. Total number of cases in the city, forty; total number of deaths, nineteen ; and of recoveries, twenty-one."

These statements may be in entire harmony with the reports made officially to the Board of Health, because, as I have said, the medical profession of the city refused to make reports to the Board of Health. But they are certainly very wide of the mark as to the real facts of the epidemic, and so are false and misleading.

Not sixteen cases, but twenty-one cases, occurred in the hospitals; and the deaths in the hospitals numbered eight at least, instead of seven.

Instead of twenty-two cases with twelve deaths, at least one hundred and seventy-nine cases were treated in the city outside the hospitals, with twenty deaths certainly, and perhaps one or two more. For I happen to know that some yellow fever deaths were assigned to other causes of dissolution; and I know also what sort of influences were sometimes used to determine the character of the certificate of death.

Sixteen cases inside of the hospitals, plus twenty-two cases outside of those institutions, would make, according to the ordinary principles of addition, an aggregate of thirty-eight cases. But the arithmetician of the Advisory Board makes out of these addends a sum equal to forty; and forty therefore let it be. Of these forty cases they tell us that twenty-one recovered, and that nineteen died; a dreadful percentage of mortality indeed. I have shown, however, that instead of an aggregate of forty cases in Mobile during the season there was really five times that number, namely, two hundred cases; and that instead of nineteen deaths we had thirty, making the percentage of mortality fifteen, instead of forty-seven and a half.

Now, it is true that the report of the Advisory Board of Health bears the date of November the 1st, although it was not published until November 27th; and that a certain number of the cases and deaths included in my statistics occurred after the first of these dates; but the epidemic was then so nearly over that corrections made with reference to this fact would afford but little help to the Board, except in the single item of the number of deaths.

The conclusion of the report is of the nature of an apology, for carbolic acid disinfection ; and an assertion, without proof of its prophylactic value.

Every step of the argument, if that may be called argument which is really no argument at all, is disingeneous and sophistical. No attempt is made to arrange the facts connected with the disinfection of the various localities which were treated with carbolic acid so as to show their bearing on the questions at issue ; but we are told in general terms that Mobile and New Orleans used carbolic acid with persistence and assiduity, and escaped any general epidemic ; and that Memphis and Shreveport and Pensacola did not invoke the prophylactic agency of carbolic acid and suffered frightfully ; and from these premises, by some logical legerdemain which passes my comprehension, the conclusion is drawn, that, *therefore*, carbolic acid disinfection arrests the progress of yellow fever. Now, in the first place, the premises are false ; and in the second place, even if they were true they furnish no logical warrant for the conclusion which is drawn from them.

With how much accuracy this Report has been prepared, may be further judged of when I call attention to one little fact of omission. The streets and grounds about the City Hospital were most elaborately disinfected. The air of the whole region was kept reeking for weeks with the foul fumes of carbolic acid, the frogs were killed in the gutters, and the grass was scorched and blasted as if the hot breath of the sirocco had fallen upon it. And yet this Report affords not the slightest intimation that any disinfection at all was practised there.

But what were the real results of the disinfection? What did the carbolic acid accomplish? The answer is short and easy, if not very elegant and refined. It made a great stink, and it did nothing else. It did not check the disease in the City Hospital. It did not prevent its migration across St. Anthony street to the Providence Infirmary. It did not keep it away from Mr. Thompson's in the acute angle between Broad street and the Spring Hill Road. It did not check its march on the Spring Hill Road along which it traveled steadily from house to house until it passed beyond Pine street, and was met by the frost. It did not interfere with its passage from the Spring Hill Road to the Shell Road, nor with its dissemination along that thoroughfare. It did not fence it out of the McCann neighborhood, nor check its ravages after it got there. In one word, seriously and deliberately spoken, it utterly failed to accomplish any good whatever ; and this is the verdict of every medical man in Mobile of whose opinion I have any knowledge. Whether it was equally impotent for evil is not so easily settled.

If we accept the statistics of the advocates of carbolic acid disinfection as at all reliable, the ratio of the mortality to the cases where carbolic acid has been used is truly appalling. Look at the terrible items as given by the Boards of Health of Mobile and New Orleans.

In New Orleans in 1871 the mortality was forty-seven and a half *per centum* of the cases.

In New Orleans in 1872 the mortality was forty-seven *per centum* of the cases.

In New Orleans in 1873 the mortality was fifty-eight *per centum* of the cases.

In Mobile in 1873 the mortality was forty-seven and a half *per centum* of the cases.

No such tremendous mortality was ever heard of before, even in the most malignant epidemics. The whole world has been filled with horror in view of the malignant energy of the epidemic in Memphis and Shreveport ; and the harvest of death which the pestilence has reaped in those stricken cities has been regarded everywhere as of almost unprecedented and exceptional character. And yet in these cities the ratio of deaths to cases reached only about one-half of the number which it reached in Mobile and New Orleans— *twenty per centum* in Memphis against forty-seven *per centum* in Mobile; twenty-five *per centum* in Shreveport against fifty-eight *per centum* in New Orleans.

In the progress of my study of the epidemic these contrasts

filled me with amazement; and I could find no probable explanation until the horrible suspicion flashed upon me that peradventure this unprecedented mortality was the result of the disinfection which had been invoked for the purpose of opposing the progress of the pestilence.

But when I saw the Report of the Mobile Advisory Board of Health and how utterly worthless were the statistics with which they deluded the public; and when, with this hint to guide me I extended my inquiries with a view of ascertaining the character of the statistics of the New Orleans Board of Health, and found that these also were entirely unreliable; then indeed I saw reason to believe that another explanation was possible; and that carbolic acid after all was not so destructive of yellow fever patients as I had supposed.

But while I am now satisfied that carbolic acid disinfection has not been the wholesale agent of destruction which the testimony of its friends seemed to prove it to be, I am very far from believing that it is entirely innocent and innocuous.

Not to go more deeply into the question, the smell of it is very offensive; and it is very easy for any one who understands the great danger of emesis in yellow fever, and the extreme sensitiveness of the stomachs of yellow fever patients, to understand also how the inhalation of an atmosphere loaded with the fumes of carbolic acid might turn the scales in doubtful cases.

The discussion of the Theory and Practice of Disinfection will be resumed in another part of this treatise. In the meantime I conclude what I have to say about the Epidemic in Mobile with a few statements furnished by several of our physicians.

SUPPLEMENTAL.

By Dr. E. P. Gaines. "The first case I had was in the family of Mr. Thompson, who lived on the Spring Hill Road, about eighty yards west of the City Hospital. This was on the 23d of September. Before the end of the season every member of this family, some nine in number, had the disease. I did not observe that disinfection with carbolic acid did any good. The fever spread steadily from house to house where it was most freely used. It was freely used at Mr. Thompson's; but the fever continued to recur in his family, and spread thence to Mr. Henry Turner's; then to Mr. Carver's; to Mr. A. J. Moore's; to Mr. Acker's; to Mr. Cieutat's. All of these places are on the Spring Hill Road, and all as they were successively invaded by the fever were disinfected with carbolic acid. Mr. Cieutat lived in the second house west of Pine street. His son died on the twenty-fifth of October. I did not hear of the fever spreading beyond this house; but I heard of two cases on the opposite side of the street. On the Shell Road the fever invaded the house of Mr. Merritt, near Pine street, Mrs. Merritt dying on the 25th of September. The premises were disinfected with carbolic acid, but the fever spread from there to Mr. J. W. Moore's about sixty yards west, where four cases occurred; and then to Mr. Julian's, whose place adjoins Mr. Moore's. The fever also passed from Mr. Merritt's to Mr. Whitfield Turner's, the next house to the east, where Mr. Dave Turner died with black vomit on the 14th of October. In all of these places carbolic acid was freely used."

By Dr. C. M. France. "On the first day of October, my first patient in the McCann family, living on Palmetto street near Marine, died. That same afternoon Dr. Hicklin, acting as Assistant Health Officer, had the sidewalk in front of the premises, the lot both front and back, as well as the house itself, disinfected with carbolic acid. It was applied so freely as to kill all the grass and vegetation which it touched. And yet in a few days another case of fever occurred in an adjoining yard, and proved fatal. The fumes of the acid were very disagreeable in the daytime, and almost insufferable at night, and continued so for weeks. In sixteen days after it was first used, four additional cases, of a most malignant type, occurred in the McCann family, of whom two died, and the other two barely recovered. At the same time other persons in the immediate vicinity were attacked with the disease, and some of them died. So far as I had opportunities for observation, carbolic acid was absolutely worthless as a prophylactic agent."

By Dr. E. H. Fournier. "I am desirous of having appended to your history of the Yellow Fever Epidemic of 1873 the following record of cases observed by me. The subjects, save one, were inmates of the City Hospital at the time of the introduction of the first case in the person of Dixon, and were confined to the house by the blockade established immediately after his death. A detail of cases which are so clearly traceable to the origin of the infection will present the type of the disease as manifested in Mobile. I have a further object also in view, and that is to add my testimony to the valuable observations made by Dr. J. C. Faget of New Orleans as to the relations between the temperature and the pulse-beat in yellow fever.

I am disposed to conclude, from my notes, that the pulse, more than the temperature, observes a fixed order of movement. This is generally a movement of recession from the beginning. Dr. Faget called attention to this fact in 1859, and has repeated it recently with the support of five hundred cases observed in Guiana and New Orleans. It is, however, in comparing the markings of the thermometer simultaneously with the count of the pulse that we are struck with the fact, not noted in other diseases, that during an ascending temperature we have a descending pulse. This relation presenting itself at the outset of the fever, furnishes a most valuable means of diagnosis.

The first case to be mentioned is that of Dixon himself, the *fons et origo* of the epidemic. He came into the hospital on the third day of the fever, with a sodden, drunken expression of countenance, hot and pungent skin, great precordial tenderness, urine scant and albuminous, pulse 90, temperature 107° Fah. Shortly after he was put to bed he ejected from his stomach a basin full of viscid fluid, which soon deposited a coffee ground sediment. The prognosis was necessarily bad. He was put upon stimulants and beef-essence. The following morning the temperature was 104°, the pulse 60, black vomit having been copiously ejected during the night. Evening: temperature still receding, and pulse becoming quicker. During the following night the patient became delirious, and died next morning.

It may be noted here that black vomit occurred when the temperature was probably at the highest, namely, 107° Fah., a degree to which this fever seldom attains, and that at the climax of the fever the pulse numbered only 90, and was bubbly to the feel. Surely the heart fails, either from the depressing influence of the intense heat, or from the more probable cause, a fatty degeneration of its substance established by the septic poison itself.

William Smith, a young German, convalescing from a malarial attack, sickened of the fever on the 17th of September, five days after the death of Dixon, and died on the 20th. His case presented the usual characteristics, the temperature not attaining so high a grade, but exhibiting the same relations with the pulse as were observed in the former case. This patient had no communication with Dixon, was not even in the large ward into which he was first brought.

Sister Xavier was taken on the 23d, and died on the 27th of September. She was not under my charge, and her case was not reported as yellow fever; but I think there can be no doubt as to its true nature, and I mention it here.

The following cases are reported more circumstantially, as the observations were made beginning with the first manifestations of the malady:

Thomas Nugent, a young, plethoric Irishman, was attacked on the 25th of September. First observation at nine o'clock, A. M. Pulse 120, temperature 103, tongue furred, bowels confined, urine copious and free from albumin, patient restless, face flushed, eyes injected and watery, head-ache and back-ache. Evening: pulse 110, temperature 104, bilious vomiting between visits, and continuing. 20th—morning: pulse 100, temperature 104, tongue red, countenance calm, head-ache and back-ache ceased, no albumin in urine. Evening: pulse 100, temperature 104°50″, skin perspiring, some nausea, bowels moved. 27th—morning: pulse 100, temperature 102, tongue red, urine albuminous, skin moist, nausea, patient calm. Evening: pulse 100, temperature 103, tongue furred and red at edges, conjunctiva and skin yellow, precordial tenderness, white vomit. 28th—morning: pulse 97, temperature 102, urine albuminous, precordial tenderness, nausea, skin and eyes more deeply tinged. Evening: pulse 97, temperature 103, restless, white vomit with specks. 29th—morning: pulse 90, temperature 101, patient calm, great nausea and precordial tenderness, black vomit. Evening: pulse 90, temperature not noted, suppression of urine, black vomit, hæmorrhage from nose and bowels. Died at 8 o'clock P. M.

This patient could not be induced to think he was sick, and persisted in getting out of bed and sticking his fingers down his throat to induce vomiting. The treatment consisted in a calomel purge, followed by quinine in large doses for the first twenty-four hours, then in smaller quantities for the next twenty-four hours, after which stimulants and beef tea.

The next patient was Louisa, a hospital nurse, who was taken with the fever on the 29th of September. First observation made at 2 o'clock P. M. Pulse 110, temperature 104, skin moist, bilious vomiting, delirious. Evening: pulse 90, temperature 102, delirious, bowels moved. 30th—morning: pulse 90, temperature 100, delirious, precordial tenderness. Evening: pulse 84, temperature 100, semi-conscious. 31st—morning: pulse 84, temperature 99, semi-conscious, stomach tender. Evening: pulse 84, temperature 99, mind clear, much prostrated with tenderness of stomach and burning heat within. October 1st—morning: pulse 64, temperature 99, rested during night, stomach tender. From this time on she continued to improve and made a good recovery, but was subject for some time to indigestion when imprudent as to diet.

The sensation of burning of the stomach was a marked symptom, throughout, manifesting itself in her delirium by her clamors for ice. Ten grains of calomel in the beginning of the attack, ice to allay the burning thirst, and applied to the head to calm the excited brain, and chloral in full doses to procure sleep, constituted the treatment during the period of excitement. This was followed, as the fever receded by stimulants and food.

Sister Mathilde was taken with chill on the 4th of October. First observation, evening : pulse 112, temperature 104, eyes and face injected, great pain in head and back. 5th—morning : pulse 88, temperature 102, less pain but oppression at the pit of the stomach with some nausea. Evening : pulse 94, temperature 103, oppression referred to head, less at stomach. 6th—morning : pulse 100, temperature 101. Evening : pulse 107, temperature 98, skin yellowish, eructations with precordial fullness. 7th—pulse 100, temperature 98, feels comfortable, stomach quiet. 8th—morning : pulse 86, temperature 96, urine albuminous, tongue dry, stomach quiet. 9th—morning : pulse 96, temperature 99, tongue moist, bilious stools. 10th—morning : pulse 100, temperature 99, skin dry, tongue dry, urine free with trace of albumin. 11th—morning : pulse 90, temperature 101, tongue moist, urine free. From this on she gradually improved, and made a good recovery. The treatment consisted of purgation first, followed by quinine for the first twenty-four hours ; then chlorine, nux vomica, phosphate of lime, stimulants and food, according to indications as they arose.

Sister Margaret was taken on Thursday, October the 16th. First observation at 2 o'clock P. M. : pulse 120, temperature 101, pain in head and back, eyes and face not injected. Evening : pulse 140, temperature 97, much nervous agitation. 7th—morning : pulse 112, temperature 101, feeling better, bowels moved, no pain. Evening : pulse 114, temperature 103, pain in head, eyes heavy with dull expression. 18th—morning ; pulse 110, temperature 102, urine free, no albumin, general hyperæsthesia, no tenderness on pressure over the stomach. Evening : pulse 84, temperature 102, stomach tender and weak, with general feeling of prostration. 19th—morning : pulse 75, temperature 100, trace of albumin in urine, feels calm, no nausea. 20th—urine albuminous, skin yellow, vomited "beeswings" during the night. 21st—urine partially suppressed and heavy with albumin, relishes champagne. 22d—feels better, pulse stronger, expression of countenance better, stomach intact. No further special observations were made. Albumin disappeared from the urine entirely on the second day of convalescence. She made a good recovery. This rapid restoration of the function of the kidneys was noticed in the majority of the cases that recovered. The treatment of the last case was very similar to the one preceding it.

Mrs. Nicholson was attacked on Thursday, the 16th of October. First observation on the 17th—morning : pulse 120, temperature 103, great pain in head and back, no vomiting or sick stomach, skin sweating and flushed. Evening—pulse 116, temperature 104, less pain in the head, restless and sleepless, no thirst, no tenderness over the stomach. 18th—morning : pulse 116, temperature 105, slept well, bowels and kidneys acting, skin dryish, no thirst. Evening : pulse 120, temperature 104, headache, vomiting bile, restless. 19th—pulse 108, temperature 102, stomach quiet, general soreness, great prostration, capillary circulation sluggish, yellowish tinge of skin. 20th—morning : pulse 100, temperature 100, urine albuminous, stomach tender, with nausea and white vomit, restless and sleepless during the night, now more quiet, no relish for stimulants or food, bowels and kidneys acting. Evening : pulse 100, temperature not taken, feels prostrated. 21st—morning : restless and weak, no relish for food. Convalescence was slow. The treatment in this case consisted of gentle laxatives, mild diuretics, phosphate of lime, brandy and beef tea.

I should mention that before the last two patients were taken, the Board of Health finding that their efforts to confine the disease to the hospital had failed of their purpose, had removed the embargo, and patients suffering from dengue, which was prevailing at the time, had been admitted. I am confident that this disease imposed some of its expressions upon the former, and altered the general course of the fever in these two cases. Witness the very quick pulse, and the subsidence of the temperature during the first twelve hours, to be re-established in one of the cases on the second day. Witness also the general soreness of the muscles on pressure at a later period. In the other case there was no complaint referable to the stomach, no thirst, and no tenderness until the third day, while there was general muscular soreness in the later period of the attack, with a decided scarlatinous eruption.

The following case was attended outside of the hospital, but within the infected district. Mr. Richardson was taken with a chill during the night of the 17th of October. Was seen first at 11 o'clock A. M. on the 18th: pulse 116, temperature 102, severe pain in head, back and abdomen, skin sweating, no thirst. Gave three compound cathartic pills, and nitrate of potash. Evening: pulse 108, temperature 104, pain in back, bowels moved. Ordered one drachm of chloral in two doses; continued potash. 19th—morning: feels better, slept some, bowels moved freely, no abdominal tenderness, pulse 88, temperature 102. Evening: pulse not noted, temperature 103, bowels checked. Continue potash and chloral, if necessary. 20th—morning: pulse 106, temperature 102, tongue red, feels weak and restless, slept some, intellect wandering, nausea but no pain on pressure over the stomach, kidneys acting, urine albuminous. Ordered phosphate of lime and aromatic spirits of ammonia, blister to epigastrium, and beef tea. Evening: pulse 100, temperature 102, urine free. Continued the same treatment, and directed brandy if the fever should subside. 21st—morning: pulse 88, temperature 100, prostrated, restless, thirst, hiccough, some nausea but no vomiting, tongue red. 22d—rested well during the night, feels better, tongue red, urine free. Continue stimulants in form of milk punch. 23d—still improving, relishes the milk punch and feels hungry. The convalescence was rapid. This individual was a subject of chronic dispepsia, and hence had a feeble constitution. He, however, passed through a very well marked attack of the fever, manifesting all of its phenomena short of black vomit, and recovered without the natural course of the disease having been altered by the medication employed. This was purposely simple. As we do not usually leave nature to her own methods of curing disease, but endeavor to direct events, we are apt to overlook the alterations, good or bad, affected by remedial agents. The tracing of the natural history of any disease without taking into account such deviations must necessarily be defective. To remedy this a large number of cases subjected to varied treatment, or to no treatment at all, should be observed. We shall thus learn nature's laws and appreciate the importance of not contravening them. By an accumulation of such facts, showing forth at the same time the true, instead of the presumed, value of remedial agents, our therapeutics will become more efficient for good. I am aware that the detail I have made presents this very difficulty to which I have alluded, but the facts recorded, will, with those adduced by others, assist in establishing upon a basis of certainty the views expressed by Dr. Faget."

REPORT OF DEATHS

Occurring from Yellow Fever, in the City of Mobile, for the year 1873.

August 26.	Owen McKenna, 117 S. Hamilton st.; age, 28 years.	
Sept'r 13.	Edward Dickson, City Hospital; 30 years.	
" 17.	Sister Mary Regina Smith, Providence Infirmary; 28 years.	
" 18.	John Young, Hospital st.; 35 years.	
" 19.	William Smith, City Hospital; 21 years.	
" 28.	Elizabeth Ann Merritt, Shell road, W. Broad st.; 61 years.	
" 29.	Thomas Nugent, City Hospital; 25 years.	
October 2.	Ellwood McCann, Palmetto, bet. Marine and Charles; 14 years.	
" 2.	Ann Scully, cor. Wilkinson and Adams; 46 years.	
" 5.	A. D. Cientat, Spring Hill road, in Pine; 6 years.	
" 7.	Dave York, Palmetto, bet. Marine and Charles; 35 years.	
" 7.	Dr. Frank M. Stone, cor. Franklin and Charleston; 36 years.	
" 9.	John D. Lanwek, Jr., Spring Hill road, in Wilkinson st.; 4 years.	
" 11.	George Smith, City Hospital; 40 years.	
" 14.	David Turner, Shell road and Broad st.; 24 years.	
" 21.	C. C. Coulton, Marine Hospital; 35 years.	
" 21.	Caroline McCann, Palmetto, bet. Marine and Charles; 33 years.	
" 25.	Ben Lane McCann, Palmetto, bet. Marine and Charles; 3 years.	
" 24.	Caroline Buttel, cor. Scott and St. Anthony; 55 years.	
" 28.	Nellie Smith, Marine, bet. Augusta and Charleston; 2 years.	
" 31.	Harmon Earle, cor. Canal and Jefferson; 50 years.	
Nov'r 8.	K. M. Cambell, Providence Infirmary; 32 years.	
" 10.	Joseph Smith, Marine, bet. Augusta and Charleston; 12 years.	
" 17.	Maria Wheeler (colored), Spring Hill road; 17 years.	
" 21.	Joshua J. Bethen, cor. Broad and Congress; 26 years.	
" 22.	Richard F. Knott, S. side St. Francis; 58 years.	
Dec'r 1.	Jacob Groeschner, cor. Warren and Church; 13 years.	

THOMAS L. GELZER, M. D.,
Reg. Vital Statistics.

METEOROLOGICAL TABLE.

DATE. 1871.	BAROMETER Mean	Bar. A.M. obs.	Bar. P.M. obs.	Bar. Night obs.	Bar. Range Highest	Bar. Range Lowest	Bar. Range Diff.	THERM. Mean	Therm. A.M. obs.	Therm. P.M. obs.	Therm. Night obs.	Therm. Max.	Therm. Min.	Therm. Diff.	Prevailing Direction	WIND Noon to 6 P.M.	6 P.M. to midnight	Midnight to 6 A.M.	6 A.M. to noon	Max. velocity per hour	Total	Amount in inches	No. of days rain/snow fell
January	30.163	30.176	30.131	30.141	30.608	29.800	.808	46.33	41.11	52.61	45.25	69	18	51	N	1908	926	997	663	28	4016	4.16	5
February	30.178	30.167	30.107	30.138	30.456	29.659	.761	56.12	50.25	62.46	55.67	75	35	40	S	1508	656	623	997	22	3599	3.15	8
March	30.199	30.235	30.162	30.205	30.708	29.730	.969	57.04	51.00	63.87	56.19	77	34	43	S	1380	696	541	857	24	4384	3.86	11
April	30.003	30.099	30.030	30.061	30.313	29.858	.495	65.67	59.83	71.46	63.73	85	44	41	S	1380	676	612	879	30	3905	0.88	8
May	29.981	29.994	29.951	29.995	30.668	29.666	.502	73.94	70.74	80.15	71.81	92	55	37	S	1413	611	377	753	24	3474	11.47	14
June	30.081	30.066	30.011	30.046	30.208	29.741	.467	79.13	76.90	83.	77.26	95	68	27	S W	1276	417	851	1032	25	2329	9.87	15
July	30.106	30.129	30.067	30.107	30.112	30.027	.185	82.15	77.96	88.54	79.80	94	70	24	S	1276	643	851	1053	32	3280	8.75	10
August	30.044	30.070	30.008	30.043	30.214	29.834	.180	80.16	75.77	88.67	78.06	94	61	33	N E	1330	835	670	739	36	3129	10.35	16
September	30.017	30.055	30.001	30.044	30.170	29.792	.378	76.16	72.11	81.76	74.46	87	34	53	N	1687	741	605	1046	16	3096	8.07	12
October	30.121	30.141	30.077	30.126	30.485	29.800	.685	65.12	58.16	72.90	6.300	74	30	44	N	1102	680	739		26	3795	1.85	5
November	30.124	30.146	30.085	30.190	30.444	29.521	.923	57.7	52.43	61.73	54.70	74	30	44	N		755	898		28	3114	3.23	6
December	30.216	30.239	30.187	30.216	30.593	29.792	.811	54.11	48.90	58.	54.53	74	28	46	N			1046		20	3801	2.07	8
Annual means	30.102	30.126	30.068	30.104	30.185	29.761	.619	66.17	61.29	72.13	64.45	84.25	54.50	18.75	S						32551	5.71	9.83

GENERAL REMARKS.

January......Changeable weather and heavy rains.
February.....Variable temperature, high winds and changeable weather.
March........Variable temperature, variable barometer; rain-fall small for season as compared with corresponding months.
April ....Steady barometer, variable temperature for the season; rain-fall very light.
May.....Heavy rains, accompanied by severe thunder and lightning; rain-fall larger than corresponding months of past years.

June......Heavy rains, changeable weather and severe thunder and lightning.
July.......Heavy rains, changeable; numerous local storms.
August.....Heavy rains; local thunder storms generally every day.
September...Local thunder storms, steady barometer generally.
October....Variable temperature; first frost noticeable on 26th.
November....Changeable weather, variable barometer.
December....Light rains, mild temperature and variable barometer.

D. O'DONOGHUE, *Observer.*

Station—MOBILE, ALA.

PART SECOND.

THE LESSONS OF THE EPIDEMIC.

Having thus given a general history of the Epidemic in several of the cities and towns, which it has visited during the year, we proceed now to the discussion of such special ques-tions connected with the general theory of yellow fever as we are able to illustrate by the facts which we have collected.

In regard to the general management and medical treat-ment of the malady, no progress of any sort has been made, and we are still under the necessity of using the same empiri-cal and expectant modes of medication as heretofore.

But without further preface, there are three special ques-tions to which I shall invite attention, namely :

The propagation of yellow fever.

The prevention of yellow fever.

The relations of yellow fever and dengue.

Upon all of which questions it is perhaps possible to say something new.

THE PROPAGATION OF YELLOW FEVER.

Of all the problems connected with the study of the natural history of yellow fever, as it presents itself in the Gulf States, none is of greater practical importance than this : Whether this fever is ever indigenous amongst us; or whether it is always of exotic origin, and finds its way to our shores only through the agency of direct importation ?

That as a matter of possibility it can be transported from place to place ; that as a matter of fact it has been transported across wide spaces, both of land and of water ; that it has in-deed been very frequently brought from foreign countries into

our own seaports, and from these disseminated to many of
our interior towns and cities; are propositions as well established as any others in the whole range of medical knowledge.
But whether it also sometimes originates on our own soil, is a
matter about which there is much difference of opinion.

Only a few years ago, and very specially during the decade
that followed the publication of the very voluminous and very
erudite, but in my judgment not very able work of LaRoche,
I think it is safe to say that the decided preponderance of
opinion amongst the physicians of New Orleans and Mobile
was in favor of the doctrine, that in these cities it was always
indigenous; that it was never imported; that, in a word, it
was the legitimate offspring of telluric and climatic conditions, and not susceptible of transportation at all.

There were some influential physicians who were the advocates of an other doctrine, namely: That while it was not of
indigenous production, not the offspring of local conditions,
that still it was not susceptible of transportation through the
agencies of human travel and commercial intercourse, but was
mysteriously disseminated over certain zones by atmospheric
or telluric waves of some unexplained character.

There existed also a general disposition to identify yellow
fever, as to its etiology and its essential nature, with our familiar paludal endemic, and to regard it as only a more malignant variety of malarial fever.

But within the last twenty years, and very noticeably within
the last ten years, the tendency of opinion on all these points
has undergone considerable change. The doctrine of the
affiliation between malarial fever and yellow fever has been
completely overthrown, never any more to be revived. The
doctrine of the transmission of yellow fever, from continent
to continent, and from city to city, by telluric or atmospheric
waves, has been pushed into the background of speculation.
And the doctrine of direct importation has been so thoroughly
established by the concurrence of multitudes of facts as to
admit no longer of controversy.

But while it is now generally conceded that this pestilential fever may be imported from abroad, and that it may be propagated along the lines of commercial intercourse, it is still contended by some that it also sometimes arises amongst us independently of foreign sources of infection. And there are two hypotheses as to how these domestic epidemics are to be accounted for. The first is, that they are strictly autocthonous—the malignant but legitimate offspring of local endemic conditions. The second is, that they are derived from the germs that have remained over from some previous epidemic —germs that have been able to maintain their vitality from one season to another, because of mild winters and other circumstances favorable to their preservation and development.

In the present state of our knowledge we are not able to say with certainty, whether either or both of these hypotheses may be either true or false. We are able to say, however, that the presumptions of contemporary writers are entirely opposed to the first ; and if the second is true at all, it is true only of one or two of our Gulf cities, and only occasionally even of them.

The problem of the propagation of yellow fever is closely associated with another problem, namely : the problem of the specific nature of the yellow fever poison. I call this poison specific, because it always produces yellow fever and never any other disease; and I call yellow fever a specific disease, because it is always produced by the yellow fever poison and never results from any other cause.

The doctrine of morbid poisons has undergone great development during the last ten years. In 1864 Dr. Beale announced the microscopic demonstration in vaccine lymph of minute glistening soft-solid albuminous particles, which he assumed to be the true contagion of vaccinnia. In 1866 he found similar microscopic particles in the infectious fluids of the cattle plague, and made the assertion that it was through their agency that this bovine pestilence was disseminated. About the same time Dr. Burden–Saunderson proved experimentally that the infectious principle of the poison fluids of the cattle plague is not dialyzable ; and it follows from this that it must be composed of colloidal matter. He did not determine whether the infectious colloid was particulate or not, but his experiments, as far as they go, are confirmatory of Beale's hypotheses. A little later Dr. Chauveau, of Lyons, conducted a very elaborate series of experiments, which are considered as having definitely established the particulate character of the contagia of small-pox, sheep-pox, cow-pox, and farcy. Subsequently Coze and Feltz, of Strasburg, made the announcement that they had been able to demonstrate also, the particulate nature of the several contagia of measles, scarlet fever, typhoid fever, and septicæmia. And later still Klebs, in a remarkable account of some observations made by him in the military hospitals at Carlesrue in 1870–71, ascribes pyæmia and septicæmia to the presence of small glistening particles of solid matter. Similar conclusions have been reached by various other observers, so that there is now a very general agreement amongst medical authorities, that the morbid poisons of the zymotic family of diseases, are albuminous, colloidal, solid and particulate.

But with reference to the specific nature of these infectious particles there is some difference of opinion.

Klebs believes that in pyæmia they are the spores of a special fungus which he names *microsporon septicum.* Coze and Feltz, and Ferdinand Cohn, and many others, teach that in all these diseases the poisonous particles are *bacteroid*; and they even distinguish specific forms among them, as *bacterium sphero,* and *bacterium catenula.*

Beale, on the contrary, holds that they are particles of the living protoplasm of the diseased organisms—particles which have undergone organic degredation and functional perversion, according to the character of the pathological movement, which serves to invest them with specific poisonous properties.

To sum up this part of the argument, without going into any detailed discussion of the intimate pathology of contagion, we may accept, as sustained by a reasonable amount of proof, the general doctrine, that the specific poisons of the zymotic diseases exist as a rule in the shape of solid colloidal particles of extremely small size, say less than the twenty thousandth of an inch in diameter; solid, and therefore ponderable; colloidal, and therefore presumably organic.

While in many directions our knowledge of these infectious particles or disease germs is exceedingly imperfect, it is well established that they increase very rapidly in numbers ; sometimes certainly within the diseased organism ; sometimes, also perhaps, outside of the diseased organism. This multiplication must be accomplished in one of two ways. Either the disease germs themselves must pass through the various vital stages of growth, development, and reproduction, and so multiply their pestiferous generations under the sun after the ordinary fashion of living creatures; or else they must through some mysterious catalytic influence transform the normal protoplasm of the organisms which they invade into germs abnormal and malignant like themselves.

The first hypothesis is the simplest, the easiest of apprehension, and was the first to present itself in the history of pathological speculation. It may turn out, however, that the second hypothesis makes the nearest approach to the truth. Of one thing, in the meantime there can be no doubt, and that is the rapid and abundant multiplication of the disease germs.

While there is good reason to believe that the infectious germs of small-pox, cow-pox, and several other eruptive diseases have been actually demonstrated under the microscope, it can not be claimed with any confidence that anybody has ever really seen the germs of yellow fever. Nevertheless we do not hesitate upon analogical grounds to affirm that such germs do exist. There is no other theory capable of explaining the phenomena of the disease.

It being admitted that the yellow fever poison is a particulate, ponderable, material thing, endowed with a certain tenacity of life, and an indefinite faculty of reproduction, it is easy enough to understand its transportation from place to place—how it can be wafted for short distances by the wind, and how it can be carried for long distances in ships, and steamboats, and railroad cars, along with dry goods, and groceries, and in the persons or the clothing of men and women.

That the pestilence in its migrations follows the usual routes of commerce and travel is certainly true. That it has never been known to make its way over any other routes than those which have been opened by human enterprise I think is also certain. In our recent epidemic, the agents by whom the infection was introduced have been definitely determined in almost every locality which was visited by the disease. There has been some question as to its origin in New Orleans; but it is at least a significant fact that the first case should occur on a vessel from Havana where the fever was epidemic at the time of her departure. It was brought to Memphis by the steamboat Bee, no matter whether the agent of infection was the boat itself, or the poor anonymous wretch who died in Riley's shanty. It was brought to Pensacola from Havana by the Golden Dream. It was brought to Mobile by Edward Dixon. It was brought to Montgomery by Mollie Jackson and Mr. Cram. It was brought to Calvert by Mr. Hughes. It was brought into the neighborhood of Greenwood by Harris F. and his brother Voss. Who can doubt that human agency is equally responsible for its introduction into those other cities where its mode of entrance has not been so clearly traced?

These facts are of very grave importance. They show beyond all peradventure of doubt that yellow fever is a transportable malady. But they show much more than this. They show that yellow fever is to be no longer confined to the seaboard, but that along all our routes of river and railroad travel every city and almost every village is annually in danger of invasion. And the more populous our country becomes and the more our facilities of rapid intercommunication are multiplied, the greater becomes the danger of pestilential visitations, and the more dreadful the consequences that follow in their train.

THE PREVENTION OF YELLOW FEVER.

In view of this state of things it becomes a question of very great importance, whether there is any way by which our people can protect themselves against these dreadful epidemics? Or whether, in spite of all our science, against the pestilence which walketh in the darkness and which wasteth at noonday, beneficient Providence has left us absolutely without defence? There are two measures of public prophylaxis which have recently attracted much attention, namely, Quarantine and Disinfection. Let us briefly consider these.

QUARANTINE.

If yellow fever is really an exotic it is then certain that absolute quarantine will guarantee absolute protection. But in this age of steamships and railroads and feverish commercial activity, and with such a spirit of reckless enterprise and adventure to deal with as is now abroad in all civilized countries, an absolute quarantine may be regarded as practically impossible. Must we, therefore, because quarantines are necessarily imperfect abandon them altogether? I think not. I think that quarantines may be so conducted that, while they would not be absolutely prohibitory of commerce and travel, they would still afford an amount of protection which would be of very great value. Such quarantines might sometimes keep the fever away altogether. Upon other occasions they might simply delay its advent for a longer or a shorter time. It might be said on these occasions that the quarantine had failed to be of any use. But it is a familiar maxim, that half a loaf is better than no bread at all; and I do not hesitate to say that if the quarantine delayed the entrance of the pestilence into any city for only a single week it would be worth many times over the amount of money it would cost to maintain it.

The difficulties that stand in the way of efficient quarantine are many and great. There are difficulties of local administration; and there are other difficulties growing out of the

imperfections of our scientific knowledge. Some of these difficulties find illustration in the history of the recent epidemic.
There was quarantine at New Orleans. The Valparaiso was
detained at the quarantine and was disinfected. There was
no fever on board and had been none. She anchored at the
wharves of the city, and in a few days her mate sickened and
died. There was quarantine at Pensacola. Nevertheless, the
pestilence broke through and devastated the city. But the
Golden Dream was detained at quarantine nearly a month.
Who shall say how much worse the epidemic might have been
if she had been allowed to approach the city immediately
upon her arrival?

Many difficulties of local administration might be consider-
ably diminished by the concurrent action of all the Gulf States
and the establishment of an unbroken line of quarantine
stations along the entire Gulf coast. But for many reasons
it would be better if quarantine against foreign countries were
under the control of the general government. It is through
the various channels of commercial intercourse that foreign
epidemics are brought to our ports; and it would seem to be
evidently expedient that the power which regulates commerce
should also have the regulation of quarantine.

Something in this direction has been done already. In
June, 1872, under a joint resolution of Congress, Assistant
Surgeon Harvey E. Brown, of the United States army, was
detailed by the Secretary of War to make investigations with
a view to "providing for a more efficient system of quarantine
on the Southern and Gulf coasts." He made his report, con-
sisting of 117 printed pages, and containing a great deal of
important information, on the 2d of December. In further-
ance of the same movement, a bill "to prevent the introduction of infectious and contagious diseases into the United
States," has been presented to Congress during its present
session, by Mr. Bromberg, of Mobile. It is well adapted to
secure the end in view, and it is to be hoped that it will be
passed into a law.

As to domestic quarantine, that is to say, quaratine established by one of our own communities against another, although it is of much intrinsic interest, I must omit the discussion of it from this essay.

DISINFECTION.

If I were writing a general treatise on the theory and practice of disinfection, I should have much to say that is more or less new, and I think important. But inasmuch as the prophylactic power of carbolic acid has been very emphatically asserted by the Boards of Health of New Orleans and Mobile, my account of the epidemic would not be complete without some examination of the question of disinfection in so far as the use of this particular agent is concerned.

I cannot discuss here with any fullness of detail the various theories of infection and disinfection, which have received the support of scientific writers; but it is necessary to call attention to a few preliminary principles such as these that follow:

That all infectious maladies are grouped together in a common class under the name of zymotic diseases, and that this class includes both yellow fever and dengue.

That these zymotic diseases are supposed to be connected in some way with an obscure pathological process, which is analogous to the ordinary processes of fermentation and putrefaction.

That low forms of living creatures are always associated with fermentative and putrefactive processes; it being impossible, however, in the present state of our knowledge, to say whether these creatures are the factors or the products of the processes in question. Take as examples here, the association of *Torula cerevisia* with the vinous fermentation, and of *Micoderma aceti* with the acetic fermentation.

That in much the same way as that which is found to obtain in these familiar cases of fermentation, living organic germs are also associated with the analogous pathological process of zymosis, the specific character of the germs differing with the specific character of the disease in connection with which it occurs.

That these organic germs, specific and malignant, miscroscopic and inscrutable, are the active agents engaged in the propagation of epidemic pestilences. They first establish themselves in colonies of inconceivable numbers in the impalpable kingdoms of the air, whence, through the mediation of the great physiological function of respiration, they invade the living bodies of men and women, in which, when the vital powers are not sufficiently strong to resist the invasion, they set up the same sort of diseased action as that with which they were originally associated, and so establish epidemics.

That inasmuch as carbolic acid and several other chemical agents, which together may be conveniently designated as antiseptics or disinfectants, are known to have the property of holding in check the ordinary processes of putrefaction and fermentation, it is reasonable to presume that they are also competent to hold in check the allied process of zymosis, and thus to prevent the multiplication of infectious organic disease germs.

That further, inasmuch as these antiseptics and disinfectants are known to have the property of destroying the vitality of many animal and vegetal organisms, it is reasonable to presume that they are also competent to destroy the organic germs which propagate epidemic diseases.

That in order to accomplish this destruction of disease germs, it is necessary that the germs in question should be brought into actual contact with the disinfecting agent, so that when the epidemic poison is disseminated through the air it is necessary in like manner to disseminate the antiseptic antidote. The principal agents employed for atmospheric disinfection are carbolic acid, chlorine and sulphur.

Such is a brief statement of the doctrines upon which the practice of disinfection is based. It cannot fail to be a matter of surprise to all thoughtful persons that these doctrines include so much that is merely probable and presumptive, and so little of positive knowledge; and it is hardly necessary for me to insist that inductions derived from such uncertain data must be received with a great deal of caution; nay, more, that they must be regarded as of very questionable validity until they have been verified by the test of experience.

Let us see, then, precisely what has been done in the way of disinfection as a prophylactic against yellow fever, and with what results. The example of New Orleans is that which is principally relied upon. It was first employed there on a large scale in 1870, when there occurred five hundred and eighty-seven yellow fever deaths. How many there might have been without the carbolic acid, it is of course impossible to say.

Yellow fever again visited New Orleans in 1871,—a memorable year in the history of disinfection. It was in this epidemic that Dr. Albers, the champion disinfectionist, put forth all his energy and exhausted all the resources of disinfection and fumigation in his contest with the fever in the Fourth District. There were one hundred and fourteen cases, and fifty-four deaths. Sixty-six cases occurred within a circular area of about fourteen hundred feet in diameter, in the center of which stood the house of Mr. Rawlings, a member of the Board of Health, and of these sixty-six cases, forty-five died. This region of infection Dr. Albers had under his own special charge. It seems to me that the result could hardly have been worse.

In 1872, in New Orleans, disinfection was again resorted to. There occurred eighty-three cases of yellow fever, and thirty-nine deaths. Of these cases sixty-one originated in the Fourth District, where carbolic acid was used with a thoroughness and pertinacity that deserved the reward of better success.

Still again, in 1873, and on a still larger scale, the aid of carbolic acid was invoked to oppose the progress of yellow fever in New Orleans. We have seen how signally it failed at every point of the line along which the conflict was waged,—how it failed in the case of the Valparaiso, in the case of the infected vessels at the wharves in the Third District, and in the case of the infected region between Chippewa street and the river in the Fourth District,—and how, in spite of sixteen thousand dollars' worth of carbolic acid, the epidemic pursued the even tenor of its way until it was met and conquered by the invincible armies of the Frost.

In Memphis, the failure of disinfection by lime, and street gas, and carbolic acid was so complete, that no attempt has been made to claim for them that in that epidemic they were of any advantage at all.

In Mobile, the account which I have given shows clearly that all the claims which have been advanced in favor of the beneficent influence of carbolic acid during our recent epidemic, are preposterous and absurd. It failed at the City Hospital. It failed on the Spring Hill Road. It failed on the Shell Road. It failed in the McCann neighborhood. It failed everywhere, and it failed completely.

In not one single instance, then—and I make the declaration with the utmost deliberation and emphasis—in not one single instance in which carbolic acid disinfection has been opposed to the progress of yellow fever, do the plain unvarnished facts furnish any solid foundation for the presumption that its influence has been prophylactic, or in any other way of an advantageous character. Very certain it is, that it has never driven away the fever from any region in which it has once obtained a footing. In New Orleans, in Memphis, and in Mobile, in spite of all the puny chemical weapons of our Boards of Health, the pestilence has successfully maintained the conflict, and continued to claim its daily tribute of human lives until deliverance has been vouchsafed to the stricken people along with the frosts of November.

But perhaps it has at least robbed the pestilence of some part of its malignant energy? Or diminished the number of cases? I think not so; and the facts which have been detailed furnish but scant reason for any such flattering conclusion. Or shall we say, that if the disinfection failed to check the progress of the fever, or to modify its type in the infected districts, that peradventure it may have restricted the limits of the infection and protected adjacent neighborhoods from invasion? This is what has been specially claimed for it both in New Orleans and in Mobile. But this claim also is utterly untenable. The argument in support of it is this : That in Mobile this last year, and in New Orleans for three successive seasons the disease was confined to certain localities, and did not on any one of these occasions extend its ravages over the whole population of either one of these cities.

But we may admit the fact, and still it does not follow that the localization and limitation was the result of the disinfection. The history of yellow fever shows that its restriction within narrow limits and quite definite boundaries, is not at all an uncommon occurrence, even when the aid of disinfection has not been invoked to account for it. In Mobile in 1843, the epidemic confined its ravages to that section of the city south of Dauphin street ; while in 1844, as if to vindicate its impartial malice, it reaped its harvest of death from the northern section of the city, the portion that had suffered the year before remaining exempt. In Memphis, in 1855, the disease was epidemic south of Union street, only a few cases occurring in the far more populous portion of the city north of Union street. In New Orleans, in 1868, the fever made its appearance in a few cases with only three deaths ; and again in 1869, there were also a few cases with three deaths. In Mobile, in 1873, as we have seen, the fever invaded forty-one different house in which no disinfection was used, to the extent of only one case in each house, no subsequent cases occurring in any of them. Illustrations of this sort might be indefinitely multiplied. I have taken only a few of those which were nearest at hand. It is manifest, therefore, that we are not warranted in estimating at any very high rate the protective virtues of carbolic acid disinfection until we have better evidence in its favor than any that has yet been adduced.

This is a question on which it is very desirable that correct and definite views should be speedily reached. For carbolic acid disinfection is certainly costly ; is certainly also exceedingly disagreeable; and in view of the appalling mortality which has on several occasions occurred in connection with it, there is room for the suspicion that some part of the mortality may be due to the carbolic acid itself. It will be well for us, at any rate, to pause in our indiscriminate praise and practice of disinfection until we are able to show beyond all reasonable doubt, that in endeavoring to suppress yellow fever we are not contributing something towards the suppression of the lives of our fellow-citizens.

I would not have it understood that I am making war upon sanitary disinfection, or upon carbolic acid. Far from it. But I do insist that the results of our costly experiments shall be correctly estimated, and truthfully reported, so that when we are hereafter threatened with pestilence we may know how much benefit is to be expected from it; and in view of all the facts which have been obtained up to the present time, I am obliged to add that the prospect of benefit in this direction is not very promising. There is a certain restricted use of disinfection by which we may hope to accomplish some good; but all attempts to destroy the multitudinous germs of pestilence which in epidemic seasons are scattered broadcast through the illimitable kingdoms of the air must be abandoned as altogether hopeless.

To disinfect all *out-of-doors* is a problem of more embarrassment and difficulty than seems to be generally appreciated. The immense extent expressed in any of the denominations of cubic measure, of the aerial space which it would be necessary to fill with the disinfectant in the form of vapor or of gas—this is one part of the difficulty. But this space being once filled would not remain filled. Its aerial contents, and along with them the vapors of disinfection would be swept away continually by the invisible swift winds and the tides and currents of the atmospheric ocean. This is another part of the difficulty. The vast amount, in pounds avoirdupois, or in gallons of wine measure, of the disinfecting material which would be necessary to supply this immense and continuous demand, day after day and week after week; and the large expense of it in dollars and cents of federal currency—this is another part of the difficulty. But suppose all these obstacles to be overcome; and that the air should be kept sufficiently saturated with the disinfectant to assure the destruction of the disease germs. It then remains to be considered whether air so laden with destructive chemical vapors would still be competent to serve the purposes of respiration—whether the same poison which proves fatal to the disease germs would not also prove fatal to human beings and domestic animals. This is another part of the difficulty,—a consideration too which is at once seen to be of cardinal importance. I venture to hope that these brief suggestions will serve to indicate the real nature of the problem of atmospheric disinfection, and what sort of an enterprise it is that we have upon our hands when we undertake the purification of the great atmospheric ocean.

As I have intimated there are some more restricted applications of the practice of disinfection from which we may still hope to derive some hygienic advantage. The disinfection of all solid articles and textile fabrics—of floors, and walls, and furniture and bedding, and all sorts of clothing, and the excretions of the sick, can certainly be effectually accomplished. This may be done by heating such things to two hundred, or to two hundred and fifty degrees Fahrenheit. Or else by the direct application of some chemical disinfectant in a solution of adequate strength. Of these chemical agents there may be mentioned the bichromate of potash, the sulphate of copper, and the chlorides of zinc and iron. Among these also there can be no question of the power of carbolic acid. In the suburbs of Mobile it killed the grass on the sidewalks and the frogs in the gutters.

The disinfection of such small portions of air as can be confined in the rooms of houses, or in the hulls of ships, would also seem to be entirely practicable. We have only to fill the designated space with the fumes of burning sulphur, or of chlorine, or of nitrous acid, or of superheated steam, and the work is done. No living creature can withstand the destructive energy of any of these agents when they are used in a sufficient degree of concentration, and with sufficient persistence.

YELLOW FEVER AND DENGUE.

It has happened upon several occasions that epidemics of yellow fever and of dengue have prevailed together in the same city at the same time, as in Mobile and New Orleans in the year just passed. The question, whether there is some generic relationship between them, has therefore assumed a a certain amount of interest. It is a question which I cannot discuss *in extenso.* I can only give very briefly the opinions I have formed in regard to it ; and I must add, in all candor, these opinions are based, so far as the nature of dengue is concerned, almost entirely on observations made in the epidemic of 1873.

I know of no other disease which has a literature in every way so perplexing and unsatisfactory as dengue. Copland has well said, that the descriptions which ·have been given of it are little creditable to their authors.

Dr. Faget, a most competent authority, is inclined to associate the New Orleans dengue of 1873, with paludal mucus fevers. In this, however, I must believe that he is mistaken. It is indeed a mucus fever, but not a paludal fever. Paludal fever, of whatever special type, is always endemic ; is always associated with paludal localities ; and is never infectious. But the dengue of 1873 presented all the characters of a true epidemic and infectious fever. As we have seen it was of very general prevalence in New Orleans. From New Orleans it spread along the coast and along the line of the railroad until it got to Mobile. Hardly a single coast village or railroad village escaped a visit from it ; and in all it was epidemic. In Mobile it was more decidedly infectious than yellow fever. It did not particularly affect malarial localities, but raged most fiercely in parts of the city where malarial fever is hardly ever known to occur. Last of all it did not exhibit malarial symptoms, and was not amenable to the ordinary treatment of malarial maladies.

I do not pretend to have made any exhaustive study of this disease, but it presented certain salient points which it was impossible to overlook. It is infectious and epidemic to begin with. It is a mucus or catarrhal fever, in the next place. Any of the mucus membranes may be involved in the pathological aberration, but very specially those of the alimentary canal, the secretions of which are dark, acrid, depraved and abundant. 1 do not regard it as a true exanthem. There is commonly more or less erythema. Less frequently the eruption is herpetic. I think it is clear that the skin symptoms are of secondary consequence, are indeed neuroses reflected from the alimentary mucus membranes—such as we see for example in *herpes zoster*.

The condition of the mucus membranes which I have indicated gives rise to copious, dark, and often offensive alvine evacuations ; and sometimes to the vomiting of dark-colored matters, which, although entirely distinct from the black vomit of yellow fever, might by possibility be mistaken for it.

The pains have one very marked feature, namely, diffusiveness. They are not confined to the head and the small of the back as is so much the fashion in yellow fever ; but there is pain everywhere, in all the muscles, and in all the joints, and sometimes in the very bones themselves ; and they are singularly persistent.

From the very beginning and through all the subsequent stages of the malady, there is a condition of extreme nervous prostration—an invincible feeling of debility and languor. I know of no other acute fever, in which, while there is so little of real danger, the apparent severity is so remarkable, and the accompanying debility so decided and so persistent. The debility indeed continues frequently for weeks, and after all the other symptoms have subsided, and makes the convalescence notably slow.

It has been said that relapses are frequent in dengue. I do not think so. I doubt, indeed, if genuine relapses ever occur in specific diseases. But however this may be, I have never seen a relapse in dengue. The type of dengue is peculiar. When fully developed it is a fever of three paroxysms. But it may be imperfectly developed, so that sometimes one, and sometimes two of the paroxysms of the normal type, may be either absent altogether, or may be so slight and transient as to escape recognition. If the attack is very slight, only one paroxysm may attract attention ; if it is moderately severe two paroxysms will be noticed ; if quite severe, there will be three paroxysms of well marked character. The first paroxysm is always most intense ; the last is always the mildest. I think the intervals are not perfectly regular. Between the first and second paroxysms, there is an interval of from one to two days ; between the second and third paroxysms there is an interval of from two to three days.

From this sketch of the natural history of dengue, it is easy to see that it is widely different from yellow fever. How any difficulty should ever have arisen as to the diagnosis of the one from the other, is something that I cannot very well understand. It is attended with much less difficulty than the diagnosis between yellow fever and certain forms of malarial fever, about which there has heretofore been so much controversy, but which is now so definitely settled. The whole physiognomy of the two maladies is different. The patient who has yellow fever is in the grasp of a giant, and he feels it and shows it. But in dengue, while the actual suffering may be greater, as it frequently is, all organic trepidation is absent. The patient feels that he is stronger than the enemy which has fastened itself upon him. I agree entirely with Dr. Faget, when he says : " It is true, that during the first twenty-four hours there is some analogy between dengue and yellow fever, but not much ; less, indeed, than there is between yellow fever at the beginning and the beginning of the initial fever of small pox." At a later period, Faget's law of the relations between the pulse and the temperature in yellow fever, becomes available as a diagnostic ; and later still, albuminous urine and black vomit, when they occur, cut all the gordian knots of doubtful diagnosis, and reveal in unmistakable language the true nature of the attack. But, indeed, there is no need to wait for these later developments. From the initial chill to the last hour of convalescence, the two diseases are entirely distinct. It is hard to describe the features of a disease in words, just as it is hard to describe the features of a a man ; but when either the fever or the man has been once seen face to face, either ought afterwards to be easy of recognition.

With reference to the effects of remedies, there are also many points of contrast between the two fevers. Of all the fevers I have ever seen, yellow fever in its initial stages is the most tolerant of large doses of quinine.

I do not stop now to discuss the question as to whether these large doses of quinine exercise a favorable influence over the subsequent progress of the disease ; but rest on the simple fact of the tolerance, which cannot be gainsayed. On the other hand, I am confident that every large dose of quinine that is taken by a patient with dengue does him harm ; and this at every stage of the disease. Even small doses during convalescence are of doubtful value.

In yellow fever, while it is considered to be desirable to unload the *prima via* by a brisk purgative at the beginning of an attack, I believe that it is generally agreed that continuous purgation is bad practice. But in dengue, continuous purgation is the best thing that can be done—purgation here, first, last and all the time, is the golden rule. The alimentary mucus membranes must be disgorged, and just as long as dark and offensive *dejecta* are obtained, the purgatives ought to be kept up

In yellow fever, the patient invariably and universally has a craving for cold drinks. Even ice itself seems often not to be cold enough to cool the intolerable burning. In dengue, on the contrary, there is but little thirst as a rule, and the patient is quite indifferent whether his drink is cold or warm, and not infrequently prefers to have it warm. For this observation I am indebted to Dr. F. A. Ross ; my own experience has completely verified it.

From what I have said, it is easy to see that in my own opinion dengue is a disease *sui generis ;* and entirely distinct both from yellow fever and paludal fever,—distinct as to its etiology, its pathology, and its symptoms ; and not less distinct, also, in the character of the response which it makes to the action of several important remedies.

Whether there is any such antagonism between yellow fever and dengue, as to cause the prevalence of dengue to oppose an obstacle against the progress of yellow fever, I am entirely unable to say. Such an opinion has been suggested, but I am not aware that it has received any definite support from observed facts. Certain it is, that an attack of one of these fevers does not afford to the patient any subsequent immunity against the other.

As to the extraordinary doctrine that dengue is a "spurious yellow fever," and the equally extraordinary doctrine that yellow fever may be modified into dengue "by the protective virtues of carbolic acid;" both of which doctrines have been asserted in Mobile during the prevalence of the recent epidemic, it is not worth while to waste time in any formal refutation of them. I imagine that after my exposure of them in the Mobile *Register;* and still more specially after Dr. Faget's tremendous criticism in the January number of the *New Orleans Medical and Surgical Journal,* neither of them is very likely to be heard of hereafter.

THE WHITE BLOOD-CORPUSCLE,

IN HEALTH AND IN DISEASE.

BY JEROME COCHRAN, M. D.,

Professor of Public Hygiene and Medical Jurisprudence in the Medical College of Alabama.

CONTENTS:

What is a White Blood-Corpuscle—Chemical Analysis—Physical Analysis—Protoplasm—The Doctrine of Cells—Digression on Amœba—The Origin of the White Corpuscle—The Movements of Leucocytes—The Physiological Relations of the White Blood-Corpuscle—The Metamorphoses of Leucocytes—The Mystery of Reproduction—The Development of the Ovum—Development of the Blood-Corpuscles in the Fœtus—Explanatory Note.

WHAT IS A WHITE BLOOD-CORPUSCLE ?

This is the first question that presents itself for solution in the course of our investigation ; and I may say of it that there is no more important question than this in the whole of the broad realm of philosophical biology.

As its name indicates, the White Blood-Corpuscle is a common constituent of the blood of animals. It will be well, therefore, if we inquire briefly into the composition of the blood ; and we may make this inquisition with reference either to its chemical, or to its physical, or to its vital constituents and properties.

CHEMICAL ANALYSIS.

In ultimate chemical analysis we know that we must find in the blood all the elementary substances which enter into t'ie composition of all the tissues and organs of the animal body; and this for the reason that the blood is the common source whence all the tissues and organs of the animal body derive the materials upon which they live and grow.

Some sixty-five elementary substances are now known to science; and of these eighteen have been found in the human body; only ten or twelve of which seem to be essential to the integrity of the organism, so that the remaining six or eight may be regarded as accidental impurities. Since elementary chemistry is only incidentally useful in the study of the phenomena of living things, it is not necessary to my purp se to make any special mention of these elementary constituents.

In proximate chemical analysis we find that the blood consists chiefly and essentially of complex compounds belonging to the class of albuminous colloids. I have made use here of a very important formula of words, namely, the expression "albuminous colloids." Let us pause for a moment, until the full meaning of it has time to find its way into our minds. What is albumen? and what is meant by colloid?

There are two principal and correlative classes of chemical substances—the class of colloids and the class of chrystalloids. You must know in a general way, that the matter which is destitute of life—the matter out of which inorganic nature is made,—is chrystalloid; that its forms are simple and definite, admitting of easy geometric measurement; that its molecules are comparatively incomplex combinations into comparatively stable aggregations of comparatively small numbers of atoms,—two or three or four, or at most a dozen or a score. You must know also that the matter which lives —the matter which moves, and grows, and thinks, and out of which is builded the bodies, fearfully and wonderfully made, of all the tribes and families of living creatures, is albuminous and colloid; that its forms of aggregation are not obedient to geometric laws; that its molecules are composed of comparatively large numbers of atoms, to be counted by scores, by hundreds, and by thousands, moulded into complex and unstable collocations: and that by virtue of their complexity and instability these colloid combinations are prone to trans-mutation and metamorphosis, are hence fluent and capable of living.

Of the organic colloids we may take albumen as the most familiar representative. It is found in almost perfect chemical purity in the white of the hen's egg. One of the simplest formulæ for albumen, that of Lieberkuhn, gives its composition as C72 H112 O22 N18 S1. This would give 225 as the number of atoms in the molecule ; and 1612 as the molecular weight ; but there are reasons for believing that the true formula is some multiple of that proposed by Lieberkuhn ; and that the true molecular complexity is therefore far greater than that which I have indicated.

PHYSICAL ANALYSIS.

The albuminous colloids are present in the blood both as soft solids and as viscous fluids, as is evident from physical analysis. Take the blood of a human creature, or of any of the higher animals, and to the unassisted sight it presents the appearance of a red, viscous, homogeneous liquid. But microscopic examination shows that it may be divided into two parts—the one liquid and the other solid ; and that these are very nearly equal, each to each, in quantity. The liquid portion consists of water and soluble albumen. The solid portion consists of granules, red corpuscles, and white corpuscles, all albuminous colloids.

The *granules* have not been adequately studied. They vary greatly in size, ranging from the one hundred thousandth of an inch, to the twenty thousandth of an inch, or even more, in diameter. Some observers have regarded them as particles of fat, some as protoplasmic masses forming the initial stages in the development of the larger corpuscles. There can be little doubt that both opinions are correct ; that some of them are of the one character, and some of the other.

The *red corpuscles* are very numerous, there being in human blood, according to the common estimate of physiologists, from three hundred to five hundred times as many of these as of the white corpuscles. Vierodt estimates 5,000,000 of red corpuscles in one cubic millimeter of the blood of a healthy man, which is equivalent to 8,000,000,000 in a cubic inch of the same blood. What unimaginable multitudes then must swarm in the fifteen or twenty pounds of blood which circulates through an adult human organism! In shape, the red corpuscles of man are flat, circular discs, with a longer diameter averaging about one-3500th of an inch, and as horter diameter averaging about one-seventh of this extent. Functionally, they are organs of respiration. They carry the life-giving and life-destroying oxygen from the lungs to the tissues.

A summary account of the natural history of the red blood-corpuscles—of their origin and destiny, and of their behavior under different circumstances, would be full of interest; but it is too large a theme for incidental treatment, and I must pass on to the proper subject of my essay, namely, the White Blood-Corpuscle, which is the last of the morphological elements of the blood in the order in which I have named them, but perhaps the first of all in real philosophic interest and importance.

The white corpuscles of human blood were first definitely distinguished from the red corpuscles by Hewson in 1777, that is to say about one hundred years ago. They are ordinarily described as spherical and granular masses, albuminous and colloidal in composition, and of somewhat greater size than the red corpuscles, being of an average diameter of about one-2500th of an inch.

You will have observed that the morphological elements of the blood have been described as of definite and geometrical shapes,—the red corpuscles as circular discs of peculiar contour, and the white corpuscles as granular spheroids. They are so described and so figured in almost all of the physiological text-books of which I have any knowledge. But such description is very far from giving expression to the whole truth; for the red corpuscles often exhibit themselves as mulberry or stellate masses; and the white corpuscles during their career of vital activity can not properly be said to have

any shape at all, distinguishable in member, joint, or limb.
Only when they are dead, or when they are quiescent under
the influence of circumstances that interfere with the discharge of their normal functions, do their soft bodies become
globular, and correspondent to the common descriptions and
figures.

As the result of recent investigations the white corpuscles
have been invested with properties and powers of such unex-
pected and comprehensive character as to necessitate the re-
vision, and even the entire reconstruction, of many of the
most important of physiological and pathological doctrines.

We know now that the white corpuscle is not simply a
geometrical solid, granular and spheroidal, except when it is
dead or dormant; that it is not a comparatively unimportant
constituent of the animal body, without any definite physiological history, and without any special work to do in the
economy of animal life. On the contrary, in current biological speculation, it has risen not simply to a position of comparative importance, but to a position in which it overshadows
all other anatomical and physiological elements. The stone
so long rejected of the builders has become, indeed, the chief
of the corner,—the foundation stone upon which must be constructed the whole edifice of the physiology of the future.

Let us see, then, if we can get some adequate conception of
what this marvellous physiological factor is.

In composition it is albuminous and colloidal. This much
we have already settled. It is a mass of living protoplasm—a
lump of animated jelly, colorless, translucent, homogeneous,
without shape, and without ascertainable structure. It is the
typical animal cell in its highest and freest development. It
eats and drinks and grows. It breathes and lives and moves.
It is obedient to the primal mandate, and multiplies its generations under the sun. In very truth it is a living creature.
It belongs to Hæckel's kingdom of the Protistæ. It is allied
to the amœbæ. *Yea, verily, it is an amœba;* but an amœba
of marked characteristics, one of which is that it has its
habitat in the fluids of living bodies, another, that it lives not

for itself but for the service of the bodies in which it is found.

In order that this summary description of the white corpuscle of the blood may be adequately understood, I must give some account of the modern doctrine of protoplasm ; some account of the modern doctrine of cells ; and some account of the natural history of the amœba.

PROTOPLASM.

Protoplasm has been defined by Mr. Huxley, as the physical basis of life. It is the living matter of living creatures ; the matter through whose agency all their tissues and organs are constructed ; the matter through whose marvellous endowments all their vital functions, such as growth, development, movement, metamorphosis, and reproduction, are accomplished. This thaumaturgic matter of life is always and everywhere of the same nature. The most refined methods of chemical, physical, and physiological analysis have not enabled us to distinguish the protoplasm of animals from the protoplasm of plants. It is soft, transparent, colorless, homogeneous, and without any of that differentiation of parts which constitutes structure. It is the same living matter that I have already described as albuminous and colloidal. But it must be remembered that some colloids are not albuminous ; and that although 'all of the albuminous colloids are closely allied to living matter, and for the most part the product of vital processes, it cannot be claimed that they are all endowed with life. It must also be remembered that not all of the matter found in living creatures is in any rigorous sense, living matter. In all those parts of the organism which exhibit recognizable structure some of the protoplasm has been transformed into something else ; something which still serves the uses and the ends of life, but which has in itself no power of motion,—no power of growth,—no power of reproduction ; and which therefore can hardly be called living.

The two kinds of matter here indicated have been distinguished by Dr. Beale, the first as *germinal matter*, and the second as *formed material ;* the germinal matter, which he also calls bioplasm, corresponding to the living protoplasm, and the formed material to the protoplasm which has passed into the structural elements of the tissues and ceased to be truly living.

The demonstration of protoplasm as the one sole form of living matter in all the kingdoms of organic nature, and the origin of all the tissues and organs of plants and of animals in the multiform metamorphoses of protoplasm, is the most important achievement of contemporary physiology. It is indeed to physiology what the law of gravitation is to astronomy; and furnishes the key to all the puzzling problems of organization and development. The discovery has been delayed for a very long time because the investigations leading to it have been attended with many difficulties. Of these, two may be specially mentioned here: first, that living protoplasm presents itself only in microscopic masses of extreme minuteness, so that the study of it is necessarily restricted to microscopic experts; secondly, that in the bodies of all living creatures, except the very lowest, it is intermingled in every variety of complex combination with the formed material of the tissues which it animates, so that it is not easy to disentangle the two sorts of matter for separate examination.

The current doctrine of protoplasm has consequently been of slow growth. The name was first applied to the soft semi-fluid contents of the vegetal cell, and especially to that portion of the contents of the most highly organized type of the vegetal cell which lies between the neucleus and the primordial utricle of Von Mohl. Afterwards the neucleus and the utricle were shown to be of the same nature with the rest of the contents of the cell, and were included under the same designation. In 1835, Dujardin applied to the simple contractile substance of those infusorial creatures which are found at the bottom of the animal scale, the name of *Sarcode*. In 1861, Max Schultze asserted the close correspondence of this sarcode with the contents of the cells of the higher animals; and his subsequent researches, together with those of Unger, Brucke, Hæckel, Kuhne, Huxley, Beale, and other workers in the same field, very soon resulted in the complete identification of the sarcode of animals and the protoplasm of plants; and in the scientific demonstration of that most prolific of biological conceptions,—that living matter is always and everywhere of the same identical nature,—the same in its chemical constitution, the same in its physical properties, the same in its vital endowments.

THE DOCTRINE OF CELLS.

Concurrently with the elaboration of the modern doctrine of protoplasm, and indeed as a subsection of the protoplasmic theory, has been elaborated also the modern doctrine of cells, and of the cellular composition of. all living structures.

The doctrine that animals and plants, however complex their organization, are still really composed of a small number of elementary parts constantly recurring, dates back to very ancient times, and was expounded with more or less clearness by Aristotle, by Galen, by Fallopius and by many others of the older anatomists. But the "simple parts" of the ancients, such as bone, flesh, cartilage, ligament, membrane, etc., do not correspond to the cells of the present day. The older observers regarded them as simple, not because they had really arrived at parts no longer analyzable, but because the imperfections of their instruments made further analysis impossible to them. It was not until the introduction of the compound microscope into the investigations of physiology that it became possible to add to the analysis of the organs into tissues, the analysis of the tissues themselves into cells. The exact date of the invention of the compound microscope is uncertain. It may, however, be stated with sufficient accuracy to have been made about the year 1600. For full two hundred years the microscope continued to be a very imperfect instrument, compared with what it has become during the present century. Nevertheless, during this time many facts were added to our knowledge of minute anatomy; and many observations were recorded which are singularly suggestive, when viewed in the light reflected upon them from the results of recent researches. For example, Borellus, of Pisa, in 1656, described pus-corpuscles as animalcules, and even asserted that he had seen them delivering their eggs! Can it be doubted, that despite the feeble powers of his glasses, there had been revealed to his earnest inquisition the same phenomena of the rapid movement and the rapid multiplication of these organisms that Dr. Beale has so graphically demonstrated by means of his one-fiftieth of an inch objective and his carmine fluid?

In 1658, Swammerdam recognized the blood-corpuscles. In 1667, Robert Hooke pointed out the cellular structure of plants. In 1670, Malpighi elaborated this subject still further. He asserted that the cells or vesicles, which he called utricles, were separable from one another, that each had its own proper boundary, and was in fact an independent entity. In 1687, Leeuwenhœk described with considerable accuracy, the blood corpuscles not only of man, but of the lower animals. He it was also who made the discovery of the spermatozoids, which he believed to be animals of different sexes; and who first announced the globular structure of the primitive tissues of the body. This globular theory was still further elucidated by Milne Edwards, Baumgartner and others, about the year 1825, and paved the way for the cell-theory of Schleiden and Schwann, which was given to the world in 1838 and 1839.

Already both the vegetable cell and the animal cell, as isolated structures, were sufficiently well known, and their importance as factors of organization had also been in some degree recognized. Schleiden was a botanist, and his reseaches are confined to the cellular anatomy and physiology of plants. Schwann applied the same doctrine to the explanation of the anatomy and physiology of animals, and proclaimed the neucleated cell as the "fundamental expression of organic forms;" that is to say, that all the tissues of all animals and plants are built up out of neucleated cells.

On account of its intrinsic interest, as well as on account of its great importance in the history of biological speculation, I add here Schwann's own statement of the theory of the spontaneous generation of cells, which is maintained by himself and by Schleiden. I quote from the Sydenham edition of his Researches :

In a cytoblastema either structureless or minutely granulous, " a nucleolus is first formed. Around this a stratum of substance is deposited, usually minutely granulous, but not yet sharply defined on the outside. As new molecules are constantly being deposited in this stratum between those already present, and as this takes place within a precise distance of the nucleolus only, the stratum becomes defined externally, and a cell-nucleus having a more or less sharp contour, is formed. The nucleus grows by a continuous deposition of new molecules between those already existing, that is by intussusception. If this goes on equally throughout the entire thickness of the stratum, the nucleus may remain solid ; but if it goes on more vigorously in the external part, the latter will become more dense, and may be hardened into a membrane, and such are the hollow nuclei." When the nucleus has reached a certain stage of development, the cell is formed around it. " A stratum of substance, *which differs from the cytoblastema,* is deposited upon the exterior of the nucleus. In the first instance, this stratum is not sharply defined externally, but becomes so in consequence of the progressive deposition of new molecules. The stratum is more or less thick, sometimes homogeneous, sometimes granulous ; the latter is most frequently the case in the thick strata which occur in the formation of the majority of animal cells. We cannot at this period distinguish a cell-cavity and a cell-wall. The deposition of new molecules between those already existing proceeds, however, and is so effected that when the stratum is thin, the entire layer, and when it is thick, only the external portion becomes consolidated into a membrane. Immediately that the cell-membrane has become consolidated, its expansion proceeds as the result of the progressive reception of new molecules between the existing ones, that is to say, by virtue of a growth by intussusception, while at the same time it becomes separated from the cell-nucleus. The interspace between the cell-membrane and the cell-nucleus is at the same time filled with fluid, and this constitutes the *cell-contents*. During this expansion the nucleus remains attached to a spot on the internal surface of the cell-membrane."

⹁ The publication of the researches of Schleiden and Schwann marks an era in the progress of physiology. In the words of Mr. Huxley, "whatever cavillers may say, it is certain that histology before 1838, and histology since then, are two different sciences—in scope, in purpose, and in dignity,—and the eminent men to whom we allude, may safely answer all detraction by a proud 'circumspice.'" Nevertheless, there is hardly a single point of their description of the genesis and structure of cells which has not been either altogether overthrown or else largely modified by the results of later investigations.

Already, in 1854, Pringsheim had called in question the necessity of the cell-wall to the constitution of a perfect cell; and Leydig, in 1856, followed by Max Schultze in 1861, defined the cell as a *mass of protoplasm inclosing a nucleus*, the cell-wall being nothing more than the hardened periphery of the substance of the cell. Bruke, also in 1861, went still further, and denied that the nucleus was an essential element of the cell, adducing in support of his opinion the non-nucleated cells of cryptogams. Shultze had discovered a non-nucleated amœba in the Adriatic in 1854; and in 1865 a non-nucleated protozoon was discovered by Hæckel in the Mediterranean, and two non-nucleated monads by Cienkowsky. Altogether, therefore, the proof is overwhelming, that cells capable of life, motion, growth and reproduction may exist without a nucleus as well as without a cell wall; and the universal conception of the simple cell as the unit of organization is now that it is an individualized particle of protoplasm, entirely homogeneous, without a nucleus, without an investing membrance, and without any recognizable structure whatever. The cells which exhibit the nucleus and the cell-wall, one or both,—and they are very numerous indeed,—are not primitive and simple cells, but cells that have already passed through a process of differentiation and development. It is only to these higher cells that the anatomical details of Schleiden and Schwann are still in some measure applicable; and at wide variance with the doctrines under examination, it is now held with reference to these higher cells, that their investing wall is caused by the consolidation of their most external portion, while the nucleus is due to a new growth of younger protoplasm within the original mass.

But no other part of this theory has been so vigorously assailed as the doctrine that cells arise spontaneously, and without the intervention of parent cells, in a structureless blastema. Already of great interest as a problem in special physiology, it has become invested with still greater importance since it has been clearly appreciated that it is really only a special phase of the great question of the commencement of life and the development of living things.

Among those who have made themselves memorable on account of the ability with which they have opposed the doctrine of spontaneous origin, or of archebiosis, to borrow Bastian's technical designation, I shall mention only two—Virchow and Beale.

In Virchow's great work on Cellular Pathology, which was published in 1858, he maintains: that the cell is the true biological unit; and that every cell is derived from a pre-existing cell, all the cells of any individual organism being the lineal descendants of the original germ-cell of the ovum; so that with him the maxim of Harvey, *omne vivum ex ovo*, becomes in its special application to histology, *omnis cellula e cellula*. Another of his fundamental doctrines is that by far the larger portion of the organism is made up out of cells derived by proliferation and differentiation from the corpuscles of the connective tissue. Still another is his doctrine of cell-territories, which I can do no more than allude to here—a doctrine which he borrowed from Goodsir.

It was in 1861 that Dr. Beale gave to the world the first definite statement of his doctrine of cells and cell-metamorphosis. He is one of the ablest of the expounders of the

protoplasmic theory, and has presented some important contributions to it, which are now very generally accepted. In
the nomenclature of the theory, also, he has made some in-
novations. The living matter he prefers to call bioplasm, and
he designates the cell as a bioplast.

He holds with the school of Virchow, that living matter,
and living matter only, can generate living matter; and that,
therefore, every cell must originate in the proliferation of some
pre-existing cell. He holds further, that all cells, or bioplasts
are in the beginning simply extremely minute, solid, homogeneous, and individualized masses of living matter or bioplasm;
and that all bioplasts grow, not by the superpo-ition of additional bioplasm upon their external surfaces, but by the genesis and integration of bioplasm in their central parts; so that
in every bioplast the central parts are always the youngest and
most vigorous; while the peripheral parts, being older and
feebler, grow continually less and less active in the discharge
of vital functions, and at last cease in any proper sense of the
word, to live at all.

But it must not be hastily concluded that this dead matter,
or *formed material* of the tissues, has become excrementitial
and useless to the organism. Far from it, indeed. For it is
out of this material which has ceased to grow, and which has
lost the power of transforming the elements of nutrition into
living bioplasm, that all the wheels and levers and pulleys,—
all the complicated scaffolding and machinery of the organism, are constructed.

DIGRESSION ON THE AMŒBA.

Many of the vital characteristics of cells or bioplasts, and
many of the fundamental phenomena of living matter may
be studied to much advantage as they present themselves in
amœbæ. Under this general name of amœba have been
classified some of the simplest of living creatures. They
have usually been regarded as denizens of the animal kingdom; but have been transferred by Hæckel into his new
kingdom of the protistæ,—a kingdom which has been erected

to include all those living creatures which have not undergone a sufficient amount of differentiation of parts to display the essential characters of either animals or plants. There are many tribes and families of these creatures ; and amongst them the amœba is one of the lowest. Yet these creatures also, so great is the variety of nature, present themselves under many different forms.

In their simpler forms they exhibit no structural differentiation whatever, not even a contained nucleus nor an investing membrane, but are homogeneous throughout. They can hardly be called organisms, because they are entirely destitute of organs. In brief, they are extremely minute masses of protoplasm,—little microscopic lumps of living jelly. Still they manifest all the essential phenomena of life. They move ; they eat ; they grow ; they reproduce their kind. They are sprawling things, without any definite or abiding shape, and go crawling about, in no particular direction, and with no obvious purpose. They thrust out any portion of their jelly like bodies into an improvised arm or foot ; and this may be immediately retracted, and another thrust out in some other direction, or its extremity may become fixed and drag the whole body after it. If they come in contact with a particle of food, mouth and stomach are improvised for its appropriation, the soft body of the creature opens to receive it, and flows slowly around it so as to inclose it completely ; and when all the nutritive material has been extracted from it, opens again, and the indigestible debris is rejected through an improvised vent which immediately disappears. If one of them is separated into any number of fragments, each fragment becomes a complete amœba;—lives and grows, and pursues an entirely independent career. Like Milton's angels, they are vital in every part, and cannot but by annihilating die. *Per contra*, if two or more of them come together they immediately fuse into one, and neither joint nor seam remains to mark the place of union. A large number thus fused together into a considerable mass constitutes what is called a plasmodium. After leading an active predatory life, for a longer or shorter time, their activity ceases and they become torpid. Under the influence of the same physical laws which mould the rain-drop, their sprawling, shapeless bodies become globular, and the external protoplasmic layer of the globe hardens into an investing membrane. Then the soft homogeneous protoplasm inside of the investing membrane undergoes a process of segmentation exactly analogous with the segmentation of the mammalian ovum during the initial stages of foetal development. But the subsequent history of the segments is different. In the mammalian ovum all the segments concur towards the formation of a single complex organism ; while every separate segment of the encysted amœba develops into an individual living creature. The segments, appearing at first in the form of simple cells, gradually assume the form of monads, and, rupturing the investing membrane, swarm out into the circumjacent water, where they soon lose their definite outlines, and pass into the sprawling amœboid type of their ancestors.

There is good reason to believe that the amœba may arise in still another way,—that it may arise spontaneously in fluids holding organic matter in solution. Take, for example, a perfectly transparent and homogeneous infusion of hay. Expose it to the heat and light of the sun, and in a few days it becomes milky and opake. The explanation of this change is that the organic matter of the solution has gathered itself into fine granular masses,—masses too small for separate examination, many of them less than the 100,000th of an inch in diameter. These granules gradually increase in size, and rise to the surface of the infusion in the shape of a granular pellicle,—the proligerous pellicle of Pouchet,—the primordial mucus of Burdach. Under the microscope irregularly shaped portions of this pellicle are soon found to undergo a process of differentiation, and these portions are then called embryonal areas. Within these areas the granules aggregate themselves into groups, which are at first of irregular outline, then become globular, and then encysted, and are ultimately developed into living amœbæ. What I have said applies chiefly to the lower amœbæ, such as the amœba porrecta, of Max Schultze; the *protamœba primitiva*, of Hæckel; and the *protomyxa* aurantiaca, of the same author.

In the higher amœbæ, such as the *amœba nuclearia*, and the *amœba limax*, there are some rudimentary evidences of structure,—namely, a nucleus, an investing membrane, and some approximation to definite shape. It seems to be well established that the lower forms of amœbæ some times undergo differential development into the higher forms of amœbæ, as, also, into the closely allied forms of *gregarina* and *actinophrys*. But into this tempting field of the transmutation of species I must not allow myself to enter. I hope that I have said enough to indicate the true character, and the biological relations of these creatures,—enough at least to show that there is ample warrant for the statement which I made a little while ago to the effect that the white blood-corpuscle is an amœba. They are composed of the same protoplasmic matter aggregated into the same elementary forms. The simple amœba is a simple cell like the white blood-corpuscle during the most active period of its existence. The nucleated and encysted amœba is a neucleated and encysted cell, such as the white blood-corpuscle becomes towards the close of its busy life. Under the microscope some forms of the amœba and some forms of the white blood-corpuscle resemble each other so nearly as to be absolutely indistinguishable.

THE ORIGIN OF THE WHITE CORPUSCLE.

Having given, as I hope, something like an adequate conception of what the white blood-corpuscle is, the next problem that presents itself for consideration is, the problem of its origin. Here it is better to widen the scope of the inquiry; and this because in discussing the origin of the white blood-corpuscle it becomes necessary to consider also the origin of certain other white corpuscles of a similar nature, namely, the lymph-corpuscle and the pus-corpuscle. Since the fact has been recognized by physiologists, that these several kinds of corpuscles are indistinguishable from one another by any analysis we are able to make, the want has been felt of a des-ignation alike applicable to them all. For this purpose the most convenient name is that suggested by Robin, who calls them all leucocytes. The word bioplast, introduced by Dr. Beale, is of still wider application, comprehending all living cells whatsoever.

There are several different hypotheses with reference to the origin of leucocytes.

1. Those who endorse the doctrine of Virchow, that cells are always the offspring of other cells, hold that the leuco-cytes which inhabit the blood are the products of the prolif-eration of other leucocytes—of other white blood-corpuscles or of lymph-corpuscles.

2. It was also held by Virchow and his school, that the leucocytes which constitute the characteristic corpuscles of pus result from the proliferation of the corpuscles of the con-nective tissue.

3. Dr. Beale and his followers teach that pus-leucocytes are also developed by the abnormal growth and proliferation of the bioplasm of epithelial cells, such as are found covering the external integument of the body, and lining the mucous membranes of the alimentary and respiratory passages.

4. In harmony with the doctrines of Schleiden and Schwann, in relation to exogenous cell formation, it has been a very common opinion among physiologists, that the several varie-ties of leucocytes arise spontaneously in the vital fluids by the coalescence of albuminous molecules. In this way the lymph-corpuscles are believed to originate from fluid protoplasm in the lymphatic vessels and glands. In this way also it has been believed, by at least a few authorities, Dr. Bastian among the number, that white blood-corpuscles are formed within the blood vessels themselves, from the albuminous ma-terials of the serum of the blood. In this way it has been believed that pus-corpuscles are developed in inflammatory effusions. And Robin has recently described with much cir-cumstantiality, the formation of leucocytes, which become ac-

tive agents in the process of reparation, in the organizable lymph which covers the surface of wounds.

5. It is a favorite speculation of many physiologists, that leucocytes are formed exclusively in the glands and follicles of the lymphatic system; and that cell-formation is the special function of these organs. Of the fact of the abundant formation of leucocytes in the lymphatic glands, there can be no question; because it has been shown that the lymph which passes from them is much richer in cells than that which they receive through their afferent vessels.

But whether the process of cell-formation within the lymphatic glands is by the proliferation of existing cells, or by the direct morphological transformation of the elements of the lymph, is entirely unknown. And while we may freely admit that these glands are important agents in the generation of cells in the higher animals, we have no warrant for the conclusion that this is the only method of cell-genesis ; and this for the reason that leucocytes are even more abundant in those lower orders of animals in which no lymphatic glands have been found, as, for example, in the amphibiæ.

It has been asserted, first I believe by His, and subsequently by several other observers, that in a very early stage of fœtal development, before the vascular circulation has been established, leucocytes are formed from the protoplasm lining the walls of the developing vessels; and Dr. Beale has suggested that a similar process of cell-genesis continues to occur during adult life.

6. In the midst of this multitude of opinions it is easy to see that the really important issue always remains the same, namely, this : Whether the genesis of leucocytes is entirely dependent on the process of proliferation; or whether it may also be accomplished by direct development out of amorphous blastemata. The process by endogenous division or proliferation, is very generally admitted. But it must be remembered that the admission rests upon purely analogical grounds, and not upon the evidence of direct observation. The proliferation has never been seen to take place. The

process by direct exogenous development, on the other hand, has met with considerable opposition, especially within the last few years, since it has been appreciated that in this controversy is involved all the principles of that larger controversy as to the spontaneous origination of living things. For myself, I have learned that nature is in the habit of using many and complex methods and agencies for the accomplishment of her purposes; and I do not hesitate to avow my belief that leucocytes may originate by any and all of the methods which have been indicated; and very specially I do not hesitate to endorse the method of formation which excludes the agency of cellular parentage.

This theory, indeed, stands upon quite as secure a foundation of facts and analysis as any other. It finds apt illustration, for example, in the account which I have given of the origin of amœbæ in the embryonal areas of the proligerous pellicle of organic infusions; and it would be easy to multiply illustrations of similar character. Take the following from the vegetable kingdom: There are several species of Algæ, such as Chara, Nitella, and Spirogyra, which consist of cyllindrical filaments, with transparent walls, inclosing liquid protoplasm. Now, under the microscope, this protoplasm may be seen to become granular; the granules may be seen to aggregate into spherical masses; and these spherical masses may be seen to become encysted, by the condensation of the outer layer of the protoplasm, thus constituting fully developed cells. If we follow the subsequent history of these cells, thus spontaneously developed in the internodes of Chara, we might find them giving issue to monads, or to amœbæ, or even to creatures of far higher type than these; thus repeating the strange drama of archebiosis already enacted in the proligerous pellicle.

THE MOVEMENT OF LEUCOCYTES.

The movements of leucocytes, as are those of all amœba-form creatures, are of two sorts; first, those resulting simply in change of shape; and secondly, those resulting also in change of place.

As long ago as 1835 the amœboid protrusion of portions of its soft protoplasmic body by the blood-leucocyte, was observed by Wharton Jones ; and similar movements were soon afterwards noted by Davaine and several other observers.

The passage of the blood-leucocytes from the blood-current through the walls of the blood-vessels was affirmed by Dr. Addison in 1841. The same fact was again described, with much minuteness of detail, in 1846, by Dr. Augustus Waller. And both of these observers declared that the extruded white blood-corpuscles were in all respects identical with the corpuscles found in pus.

They failed, however, to grasp the conception that the leucocytes were endowed with independent amœboid vitality and the faculty of spontaneous locomotion. They were consequently unable to give a rational explanation of the phenomena of which they were the first witnesses. They stood upon the threshold of the discovery which has revolutionized both physiology and pathology ; but with the doors of the temple of life wide open before them, they saw nothing but shadows. Their observations bore no fruit, and very soon fell into oblivion.

I have shown how one revolution in histology followed the application of the compound microscope to physiological research. The new revolution of which I am now speaking followed also upon the introduction of improved methods of investigation. Of these by far the most important is the substitution which has been so largely made of the living tissues and fluids in the place of their dead remains as the objects of physiological and pathological study. The living elements of the tissues, and especially those in which the vital functions are most active undergo great changes in the very act of dying, and are still further altered by immersion in water and acetic acid and other fluids, and by the various manipulations that have been employed as the preliminaries of microscopic examination ; so that it is easy to see that if we would know organic forms in their organic integrity we must study them while they are still living.

The importance of making the living tissues themselves, under the various conditions and circumstances of real life, the basis of histological study was never indeed entirely overlooked, nor greatly underrated. But the difficulties attending this sort of study were almost insuperable, until within quite recent times they have been in some measure overcome by the employment of curare and chloroform. The first of these agents enables us to paralyze the nerves of voluntary motion ; the second enables us to paralyze the nerves of sensation ; while both of them leave untouched all the great functions of organic life, such for example, as respiration, circulation and nutrition. In this way by abolishing at the same time the power of motion and the sense of pain in the creatures subjected to examination, some of the cardinal obstacles which stood in the way of histological discovery have been removed, and many things have been seen face to face which before were visible only as through a glass darkly.

The complete and final demonstration of the amœboid endowments of leucocytes was made by Professor Von Recklinghausen, and was published by him in a paper on suppuration which appeared in 1863. In this memoir Von Recklinghausen established on a firm basis the following propositions :

1. That leucocytes exhibit rapid amœboid changes of form.

2. That leucocytes possess the power of moving from place to place through the meshes of the soft tissues.

3. That leucocytes are capable of flowing around minute solid particles of any kind so as to imprison them completely or partially in the soft protoplasm of their amœboid bodies.

The amœboid changes of form were established by observations made on pus-corpuscles which were found in the aqueous humor of the anterior chamber of the eye of a frog a few days after keratitis had been excited by irritation of the cornea. I add here the account of what he saw in his own words :

"The corpuscles differ very strikingly in their form from those from which the ordinary descriptions are taken. * * *

No globular forms present themselves,—only jagged ones, and the prongs vary both in length and number. But what strikes one even after very brief examination is, that each corpuscle is constantly changing its shape. While one prong withdraws itself into the body of the corpuscle, another juts out. Each prong is at first a delicate, homogeneous, somewhat slimy thread; but it soon thickens at the base, lengthening at the same time. Then gradually the substance of the corpuscle tends more and more towards it, becoming smaller as the process gets larger, the whole thus assuming an oblong or protracted form. During this transformation the tip of the process is rounded off and subsides into the contour of the corpuscle; or new thread-like processes shoot out and again undergo the same changes."

The ingestive power of the leucocytes was proved by a variety of experiments. One method was by the introduction of milk into the lymph-cavities of frogs, the result being that the corpuscles of the lymph or white blood of these creatures became choked with milk-globules. Another method was the injection of finely divided vermilion into these cavities. The vermilion was speedily absorbed by the leucocytes with the effect of course of imparting to them a red color. This method of feeding the leucocytes with insoluble pigments injected into the circulating fluid affords a ready means of marking the blood-leucocytes, so that they may be distinguished from those which are indigenous to the tissues.

The proof of the faculty of locomotion in the leucocytes was derived from such experiments as these:

The lymph-cavity of a frog was injected with vermilion so as to color the leucocytes. The cornea of a rabbit, or of a dog, was then introduced into it, and allowed to remain for two or three days. The lymph-sac of course became inflamed, and the fragment of cornea was found to have grown turbid in its superficial portions, the central parts still retaining their natural transparency. Microscopic examination showed that the turbidity was due to the presence of amœboid leucocytes in the dead tissue; and that these leucocytes were derived by immigration from the purulent lymph in which the cornea had been immersed was evident from the fact, that they were living and moving, that they contained particles of vermilion, and that they agreed in size and other characters with the leucocytes of the frog.

In this little historical sketch it is important to remember that Von Recklinghausen's researches were confined to the leucocytes of pus. His experiments were repeated and varied by many observers, with the result that abundant confirmation was brought to sustain his conclusions.

For example, Lortet of Lyons, found that if any porous substance is introduced into a suppurating cavity, the leucocytes penetrate into it in the same way as they do into the dead cornea; and that if the swimming bladder of a small fish, filled with water, is introduced into an abscess, the enclosed fluid soon becomes peopled with leucocytes.

The next important step in this investigation was made by Cohnheim, who in 1867 announced the migration of blood-leucocytes, during the earlier stages of inflammation, through the walls of the bloodvessels into the adjacent tissues. I proceed to give some account of the experiment by which this immigration was demonstrated.

A male frog, which has been paralyzed by the injection under the skin, of about the one-2000th of a grain of curare, is secured on a plate of glass. A vertical incision is then made through the abdominal wall, extending from the lower edge of the liver downwards to the extent of half an inch; and so much of the small intestine is drawn out of the visceral cavity as is necessary, in order that the mesentery may be evenly spread on a disc of glass, which is fixed in a convenient position for the purpose. After an interval of some hours the exposed peritoneum begins to inflame. First there is increased activity of the capillary circulation. Then follows the stage of the retardation or slowing of the blood-current; and simultaneously with this the leucocytes begin to crowd against the vascular walls, until the veins become lined with a continuous pavement of these bodies, which remain almost motionless, notwithstanding that the axial current still sweeps along. Now is the time when the migration is likely to commence, and it is necessary to select some particular vessel for observation. Upon the outer contour of this vessel spring out minute, colorless, button-shaped elevations, just as if they were produced by the budding out of the wall of the vessel itself. The buds increase gradually and slowly in size, until each assumes the form of a hemispherical projection of a width corresponding to that of a leucocyte. Eventually the hemisphere is converted into a pear-shaped body, the stalk-end of which is still attached to the surface of the vein. Gradually the little mass of protoplasm removes itself further and further away, and as it does so, begins to shoot out delicate prongs of transparent protoplasm from its surface, in no wise differing in appearance from the slender thread by which it is still moored to the vessel. Finally this thread itself is severed and the process is complete. The observer has before him an emigrant leucocyte in all respects similar to those which have been already described in the aqueous humor of the inflamed eye.

This description of the migration of the white blood-corpuscles through the walls of the bloodvessels, which is given almost in the very words of Cohnheim's account of his observations on the frog's mesentery, is almost identical, even in its details, with that of Waller, twenty years before, of his observations on the frog's tongue. And yet the fame of Cohnheim's discovery has resounded to the ends of the earth, while Waller's never attracted any serious attention and was at once forgotten. The explanation is easy. Waller was ahead of his time. The verification of the fact which he announced was difficult; it could not be put to use; there was no place for it in any of the current schemes of physiological speculation. No wonder then that the discovery fell stillborn. When Cohnheim's investigations were made all the circumstances had been changed. The announcement harmonized with many established opinions, and met with comparatively easy and abundant verification.

Accepting, then, the amœboid character and the extravascular migrations of the white blood-corpuscles as definitely established, we proceed next to inquire into the nature and extent of their agency in physiological and pathological processes.

As to the migration of the blood-leucocytes, it will be observed that it has been seen to occur only in the initial stages of inflammation, that is to say, as a pathological process. Does it also occur as a physiological process under the ordinary conditions of growth and development? This question must be answered in the affirmative ; because there are many facts to warrant the affirmation, and because it is a well established principle that pathology is only abnormal physiology,—that the condition of disease is not a radically different condition from that of health, but simply a prolongation higher or lower of the actions proper to the normal organism.

THE PHYSIOLOGICAL RELATIONS OF THE WHITE BLOOD-CORPUSCLES.

Here again we have reached a station at which it becomes expedient to widen the field of discussion.

We have learned already that blood-leucocytes are individualized particles of living bioplasm ; that in very truth they are *quasi* independent living creatures, endowed with all the vital faculties of the simpler amœbæ, including the faculty of spontaneous locomotion ; that on account of their frequent community of origin and of destiny, and of their invariable community of character, the study of them cannot be separated from the study of the leucocytes of lymph and of pus.

Let us now learn that they are also of the same identical nature with the germinal vesicle, with the segmentation-spheres of the developing ovum, and with the so-called cells of the blastodemic layers of the embryo, out of which are developed all the tissues and organs of all the higher orders of animal creatures, and it will be seen that I had ample warrant for the assertion that the stone so long rejected of the builders, was become the chief of the corner,—that it was upon the foundation of the white blood-corpuscle that the physiology of the future was to be constructed.

The problems involved in this division of our subject can be presented to the greatest advantage in a general discussion of the metamorphoses of leucocytes. To this we will accordingly proceed.

THE METAMORPHOSES OF LEUCOCYTES.

At a previous stage of this inquiry, we found it expedient to substitute for the term "white blood-corpuscle," the more compact and comprehensive term, "leucocyte." Now that we have reached a still higher generalization, it becomes again convenient to change our nomenclature. Hereafter, therefore, we will use in place of the word "leucocyte," the more general expression introduced by Dr. Beale, namely, "bioplast." We have, then, to designate the science of living creatures, the term Biology; to designate living matter, the term Bioplasm; and to designate any individualized particle of living matter, the term Bioplast,—a nomenclature which is at once consistent, convenient, comprehensive and suggestive.

We are now ready for the discussion of the metamorphoses of bioplasts,—that is to say, for the discussion of the genesis, the growth and development of living tissues, and of living creatures, for all these questions will be found to be involved in the metamorphoses of white blood-corpuscles, or of their biological equivalents.

By the growth of a living creature we mean that there is an increase in its size, that is to say, in the quantity of living matter which it contains. In analyzing the processes of growth there are three things to be considered, namely:

1. The living creature itself which grows. This may be a creature whose whole body consists of a single microscopic mass of bioplasm—a single bioplast without organs or tissues. Or it may be a creature compounded of many millions of bioplasts or cells arranged into many complex tissues and organs. But in all cases the act of growth is essentially the same. Each individual bioplast, whether living alone or colonized in a complex organism, appropriates for itself, by

the exercise of its own vital powers, the food upon which it lives and grows.

2. The food or pabulum which is appropriated in the process of growth,—the materials out of which the bioplast constructs the very substance of its own body. The cardinal fact of the process of growth is this, that the act of appropriation of food is an act of transformation. The bioplasm is always of a different nature from the food out of which it was made. The elementary constituents of the food,—the carbon, the hydrogen, the oxygen, the nitrogen, the sulphur, these indeed are not changed; but their molecular arrangement is changed and the amount and character of the change is not always the same. Plants, which contain chlorophyll, are able to transform into bioplasm the inorganic gasses of the atmosphere; while the highest feat of constructive chemistry of which animals, which contain no chlorophyll, are capable, is the transformation into bioplasm of the albuminous colloids. In either case matter which is not living is metamorphosed into matter which lives.

3. The products and sequences of the process of growth. The bioplast which grows increases in size; and this increase of size results from the addition to its mass of new bioplasm. It is important to remember, what has been stated before, that the new bioplasm is not added to the surface of the growing bioplast by superposition; but it is added to the central parts by intussusception; so that the outside parts of the bioplast are always oldest,—are always growing senescent, while the central parts exhibit the plasticity and energy of youth. Again, as the food passes by metamorphosis into bioplasm, so the bioplasm in its turn passes by another metamorphosis into the formed material—the structural elements of the tissues and organs. This formed material which first appears on the periphery of the bioplast does not itself grow, but increases by the superposition on its internal surface of other formed material derived from the metamorphosis of other bioplasm. Last of all, the formed material itself undergoes

metamorphosis,—disintegrates and passes back into the realm of inorganic nature.

THE MYSTERY OF REPRODUCTION.

The most fundamental metamorphosis then of a bioplast is its metamorphosis into formed material—into histogenetic elements. But this metamorphosis is not universal. There are many bioplasts which pursue an entirely different career,—which undergo metamorphosis by the division of their bodies, and thus become instrumental to the process of genesis, generation, reproduction,—the process by which the multiplication of bioplasts is accomplished.

The whole mystery of reproduction, in all the kingdoms of organic nature is found here in the division of a bioplast,—in the separation of one microscopic mass of living matter into two microscopic masses of living matter, for this is, in very fact, the separation of one living creature into two living creatures. The relations existing between growth and genesis are of the most intimate kind. Indeed, in ultimate analysis they are but two phases of the same vital process. Growth is continuous development. Genesis is discontinuous development.

We have seen that the multiplication of the lower amoebæ is accomplished by two apparently different processes. But a little examination shows that the two processes are really of the same essential character, taking place under the influence of different circumstances, and differing only in nonessential details. Both are processes of segmentation—that is to say, of single division. When the amoeba is young, and its entire mass is composed of growing bioplasm without any peripheral envelop of formed material, the segmentation involves the outside as well as the inside of the mass. But when the amoeba is older, and has become enveloped in a layer of matter which has ceased to live, then the segmentation is confined to the living bioplasm within the envelop.

Here, in the primitive type of the reproductive process, there is no such relation between successive generations as that of parent and offspring. The young amœba has neither father nor mother. One living creature has not produced another living creature, retaining at the same time its own individuality unimpaired; but one individual has passed entire with all its parts and powers, into several segments, each of which is a new individual.

When we get a little higher up in the organic hierarchy, among creatures of larger size and more complex construction, the genesis of new individuals is still accomplished by segmentation; but in these the segmentation is partial instead of general,—that is to say, the division does not destroy the individual identity of the creature which is divided. Here we might in some intelligible sense speak of parent and offspring. But at first, and through primitive types innumerable, the parent is neither father nor mother, and the offspring are neither sons nor daughters. As yet there is no sex.

Reproductive segmentation may be either external or internal. In the case of external segmentation a bud grows out from some part of the external membrane which envelops the body of the parent, and in due time is thrown off and left to shift for itself. In most of these cases the segmentation is necessarily external, because most of these creatures have no cavities in their bodies, and consequently no internal membranes which can give origin to internal segments.

But as soon as, in the ascending scale of living things, we arrive at creatures containing cavities in their bodies, it is within these cavities, and upon their lining membranes, that the segmentation occurs.

The change from external segmentation to internal segmentation, is not of so radical a nature as at first it appears to be. The internal membranes are only infolded portions of the external membranes,—are, in other words, only portions of skin which have dipped down into the visceral cavities. These membranes, both internal and external, are covered with epithelium,—with epithelium variously modified and differentiated according to circumstances, that is to say, according to the action of incident forces. And this rule holds good down to the smallest glands and follicles which open upon the skin, or upon any of the mucous surfaces. The mucous membranes, being thus mere involutions of the skin, are, in all essential particulars, of the same character with it. But inasmuch as they are softer than the skin, more permeable to the elements of nutrition, and more protected from adverse influences, they present more favorable conditions for the outgrowth of the reproductive buds or segments. It is for this reason that nature, always parsimonious and wisely frugal of her resources, selects these internal membranes as the instruments and agents of 'reproduction. And this stage of animal development being once reached, internal gemmation, internal segmentation, internal reproduction becomes henceforth the invariable rule.

And this little bud or segment, which is the beginning of a new creature, what is it? and whence is it derived? It is a little mass of bioplasm; and it is developed from one of the epithelial elements. In other words, it is a bioplast resulting from the metamorphosis of an epithelial cell. But what then is an epithelial cell? This also is a bioplast which has undergone a special metamorphosis. And whence this marvelous bioplast, which is the common germ alike of epithelial cells and of living animals? In the present state of physiology, its genealogy cannot be very confidently given. But more and more there is a disposition to accept the doctrine propounded long ago by Dollinger, and more recently by Biesiadecki,—the doctrine, namely, that the epithelial cell is derived by simple metamorphosis from the wandering white blood-corpuscle. And if the epithelial cell is derived in this way from the white blood-corpuscle, why then it is plain that the white blood-corpuscle is the immediate ancestor of every living creature; yea, verily! that man himself, fearfully and wonderfully made, is but an infinitely developed migrating leucocyte.

If it should be objected that Biesiadecki's doctrine of the origin of epithelium is not yet definitely established, this much at least remains certain, namely: That the epithelial cell and the migratory leucocyte are of the same essential character, —are both microscopic masses of individualized bioplasm,— are, in a word, biological homologues. In the meantime, the doctrine that every living creature begins in an epithelial cell,—in a bud springing from an epithelial surface, is no longer open to question. And why should this be considered an incredible theory,—an absurd and fanciful physiological dream? It has the support not only of observed facts, but of all the *a priori* presumptions of biological science. The bioplast is the biological unit, the fundamental element of organization. It is therefore the natural and inevitable starting point of every living organ and of every living organism.

It is in the sub-kingdom *Cœlenterata* that permanent cavities first appear, and it is here, consequently, that internal segmentation is first manifested. The permanent cavity of cœlenterate animals is known as the gastro-vascular cavity. Let us understand clearly what is meant by this. In these animals but little progress has been made in the differentiation of organs and functions. They have no vessels for the circulation of the blood; indeed, they have no blood to circulate; but they have a many-chambered, branching cavity which serves at the same time for the ingestion and the digestion of food, and for the distribution of the nutritive fluid. This is the gastro-vascular cavity. It is lined, of course, with epithelium. Now, in the lower *Cœlenterata*, the entire reproductive apparatus consists of a few spots on the surface of the walls of this cavity. These spots are covered with a sort of epithelium, which is known as germ-epithelium, the cells of which, by simple growth, become developed into eggs.

In the higher *Cœlenterata* the process of differentiation has taken another step in advance. The germinal spots sink down into the thickness of the walls of the cavity, so as to form epithelial follicles or sacks. Within these follicles the eggs are developed as before, by the simple growth of the epithelial elements. When mature they are discharged into the gastric cavity, and thence find their way into the external world.

We have thus traced the process of reproductive gemmation, or segmentation, or ovulation, as far as is necessary for
the purpose which we have in view. It is true, that we have
only reached the borders of the animal kingdom, the *Cœlenterata* being the first creatures in the ascending scale of development, which are distinctly and unmistakably animals.
But the type of ovarian development which they present,—
that of *an* epithelial follicle gland, is substantially repeated *or*
through all the higher classes and orders up to man. There
are variations almost innumerable, of special form and loca-
tion, and of accessory and supplemental organs and appenda-
ges; but the type of the epithelial sack is never changed.
Away up among the higher orders of *Vertebrata*, the open
epithelial sack of *Cœlenterata*, *Annulosa* and *Molluska* is replaced by a closed sack. But as this is still lined with epithelium, and is occasionally opened for the discharge of eggs
or germs, it is really only a modification and not a change of
the type.

In the human female the ovaries are developed in connection with the *corpora Wolfianœ*. They are the homologues
and the analogues of the testes of the male which are also
developed in connection with the *corpora Wolfianœ*. In the
beginning of their development, they consist of a mass of fibrous stroma, which is well supplied with bloodvessels and
covered over with a layer of cylindrical epithelium. This
epithelium is also called ovarian epithelium, and germ-epithelium. As the development goes on, some of these epithelial cells are seen to be larger than others, and it is these
which are to pass by metamorphosis into the future eggs.
Very soon processes of the fibrous stroma shoot up above
the general level, while the epithelial membrane sinks down
into the depressions between them. The processes continuing to grow, we have presently deep, open follicles lined with
the germ-epithelium, such as we have already seen in *Cœlenterata*. Each of these open sacks sinks continually deeper
and deeper into the underlying stroma, while the uprising
processes approximate more and more until at length they

touch and adhere together, and the mouth of the sack is closed by their adhesion. This closed sack is the follicle of Von Graafe. Within it the development of the ovum and its envelops gradually proceeds to completion, all of its various parts being derived from epithelial elements.

Inasmuch as we have found the typical ovarium fully developed in creatures like the *Cœlenterata*, which stand at the very beginning of the animal hierarchy, we would expect, in accordance with the principles of transcendental physiology, to find this organ in the higher animals presenting itself at a very early period of fœtal development. And such is really the case. While the fœtus as yet exhibits no signs of human structure, but is still of the soft, larval, and *quasi* cœlenterate type, the ovaries, with the Graafian follicles and the ova are all to be found in a state virtually complete. The female infant comes into the world with her ovaries full of eggs,—that is to say, full of the germs of future human creatures. Nature, usually so parsimonious, makes prodigal preparation for the continuance of the race. The number of ova in the ovaries of a single human female is immense. It has been estimated at as high a rate as four hundred thousand. Of these myriads very few comparatively, perhaps not more than from three hundred to five hundred, ever escape from the follicles in which they were formed; and of those that do escape very few are ever developed into living human beings.

I shall not pause to describe the minute anatomy of the human ovum. The truly essential portion of it is the so-called germinal vesicle. This is a particle of living matter,—a microscopic bioplast, and therefore entirely analogous to the white blood-corpuscle. When mature it contains a nucleus and therefore is a bioplast which has reached a comparatively high stage of development.

As we have already seen the *testes* of the male are both homologous and analogous with the ovaries of the female,— that is to say, their structural relations are the same, and they are appropriated to the discharge of corresponding functions. The spermatazoon is both homologous and analogous with the ovum. It is a metamorphosed cell,—the product of the metamorphosis of an epithelial cell, or at any rate of a cell which under other circumstances would have assumed epithelial characters. It is called a seminal cell, and is neucleated like the germinal vesicle. The nucleus forms the head of the fully developed spermatozoon, while the rest of the bioplasm of the cell sprouts out to form the tail; so that the whole substance of the seminal cell is to be found in the spermatozoon. There has been a change of form, and with this the acquisition of new functions. The spermatozoon is therefore very closely related to the white blood-corpuscle.

I cannot enter here into any adequate discussion of the transcendental mystery of sex ; but it will not be amiss, perhaps, if I make two or three summary suggestions towards the reduction of the problem to its simplest terms.

What is it that takes place in the act of sexual impregnation? Simply this : Two bioplasts, endowed with different faculties, although closely allied in their physiological history, *are fused into one.* Everywhere the process of sexual conjugation, when stripped of the glamour of mystery and ceremonial with which Nature for wise purposes loves to invest it, has this for its object,—this fusion of two microscopic cells into one.

I said, just now, sexual conjugation ! But the conjugation and fusion of cells, as occasional stages in the drama of reproduction, occur very frequently in creatures in which no distinction of sex can be recognized. Take an example or two.

In Desmids and Diatoms, which are unicellular aquatic plants, multiplication usually takes place, by simple duplex subdivision. But occasionally a different plan of reproduction is invoked. Two of these single-celled creatures come together so as to touch one another, it may be by accident, or it may be, as I believe that it is, as the result of some mysterious and reciprocal organic attraction. The walls of the two cells first grow together at the point of contact ; and then the partition thus formed is broken down, and the contents

of the two cells become commingled into a single homogeneous mass of bioplasm. Around this there is soon formed a
cellulose envelop, and we have a spore which serves as the
starting point of a new series of proliferating cells.

In *Spirogyra*, a genus of fresh water algæ, we find another
illustration of cell-conjugation of essentially the same character, but differing a little in some of the details. These
plants consist of slender green filaments formed of single
rows of cylindrical and elongated cells. Between the cells of
two adjacent filaments a wonderful attraction is sometimes
seen to manifest itself. In their eagerness to embrace one
another the wall of a cell in one filament bulges out to meet
a corresponding protrusion of the wall of a cell in another
filament; the two protrusions come into contact; the intervening walls are absorbed; the whole of the bioplasmic contents of the two conjugating cells are gathered into one of
them; and a spore is thus formed, which in due time germi-
nates into a new plant.

Again. We have seen how several previously independent
non-nucleated amœbæ may become associated together in a
plasmodium, which in time may become encysted and by segmentation give rise to new generations of amœbæ. Is this,
als·, an example of reproductive conjugation?

Now here among the lowly creatures which have furnished
these examples of conjugation, there is neither male nor
female. The conjugating cells are exactly alike. And yet we
have here substantially the same physiological results as those
that follow the sexual conjugation of the higher plants and
animals. We have the mysterious fusion of two cells into
one cell,—of two bioplasts into one bioplast, to form the germ
out of which a new creature is to be evolved. In other words,
we have manifested here among creatures in which no sexual
differentiation has been established, that very same process
of conjugal reproduction for which the agency of sex is ordinarily invoked as the only possible explanation. It is easy
enough to say that this is practically the same thing as the
assertion of the real existence of sex in creatures which ex-

hibit no recognizable sexual characters. And I have no doubt that this is frequently the case. But I believe that in those first and simplest conjugations which occur in the very lowest ranks of organic life, there is no intervention of sex at all,— either of sex actual, or of sex potential; but that the conjugating cells are really, as they seem to be, of the same nature, or, to speak paradoxically, of the same sex,—that is to say, of no sex at all. On this presumption, sex, like all the other faculties of living things, arises by imperceptible gradations out of a common basis of homogeneous bioplasm, in obedience to the general law of organic evolution, through the ordinary processes of growth, development, and differentiation. The diversity, which at length becomes so great, is developed out of a unity which is well nigh absolute.

Let us see, if we can, what it is that really takes place in that wonderful conjugation of bioplasts which is instrumental in reproduction. In the first place, it is evident that conjugation does not belong to the essence of the act of reproduction; and this for the quite sufficient reason that we have found reproduction to take place abundantly without it. Clearly, then, conjugation is not a primitive factor in the process of reproduction. It is only a secondary, an accessory, a supplemental factor.

But what, then, is its special purpose? In what way does it reinforce and supplement the fundamental forces of reproduction? In order that we may find the answers to these questions, we must study the special circumstances under which its agency is invoked. We have seen already that reproduction, in its simplest, in its most primitive, in its truly essential forms, is nothing more than an incident of growth. When growth is continuous we have increase of size,—part is added to part. But growth is sometimes discontinuous; the individuality of the growing mass is destroyed, so that it falls asunder, part from part, and each part becomes a new individual and leads an independent life.

Now this falling asunder of the growing mass,—this curious phenomenon of discontinuous development, occurs during the larvel condition of the creature that divides,—that is to say, while the processes of growth are specially vigorous and active. But when the growing mass has reached maturity, and the activities of nutritive life are diminished or suspended, then also, this sort of multiplication is diminished or suspended, and the act of reproduction can be accomplished only through the supplemental agency of conjugation. This supplemental agency of conjugation, then, restores the reproductive or proliferative energy which has been lost through the waning of the powers of growth—of development—of evolution. It always does this. But as we ascend the scale of organic life it is found to do almost infinitely more than this. Its office is magnified more and more the higher we get,—is, indeed, at length so immensely magnified and so variously differentiated, that it is not strange that its original character should be overlooked.

It restores to the senescent and languishing creature, or to some of its segments, its waning power of growth and development. Restores it, but how? The answer to this question even, is not beyond all conjecture. The subsidence of the power of growth and development is concurrent with the establishment of equilibrium among the forces that minister to nutrition. All motion, of whatever character, depends upon some disturbance of equilibrium. In mechanics the complete equilibrium of all the mechanical forces is equivalent to complete rest. In physiology the complete equilibrium of all the vital forces is equivalent to death. Now the fusion of two bioplasts into one in the act of conjugation, breaks up, in the most thorough manner, the paralysis of equilibrium which is stealing over them both, and in the complex mass which results from this union, sets all the wheels of life into active motion.

One of the most curious questions connected with sexual generation, is this : Which is physiologically the real parent of the child, the father or the mother ? There can be no hesitation as to the answer. Beyond all question the child is, in a very special sense, the offspring of the mother. Swedenborg tells

us that the body and animal life of the human child are derived from the mother, but that the soul is furnished by the
father. The doctrine of the natural generation of the soul
has been condemned by the church; but there is a sense in
which this conception of the Swedish seer becomes exceedingly suggestive. I cannot dwell upon it, however, now.

Sometimes, very frequently, indeed, even among creatures
that are truly sexual, the new individual has but one parent;
and invariably this solitary parent is of the female sex.
Hence this sort of reproduction has been called Parthenogenesis. In the common plant-louse—the *aphis*, for example—
when the weather is pleasant and food abundant, a very rapid
process of multiplication goes on without any assistance from
the male insect. During this time, indeed, the offspring as
well as the parents are all females. For generation after generation no males are to be found. But when the conditions
of existence become more stringent, when food is hard to get
and the weather is unpropitious, and life really becomes a
struggle, then the male animal makes his appearance, and
the aphide mothers are no longer virgins. We have seen how
the ovum makes its appearance in the female foetus of the human race while the foetus itself is still within the womb of its
mother. The same thing takes place in all the higher animals; perhaps, also, in all the lower animals. At any rate, it
has been observed in the organic reproduction of *aphides*,
which I have just described. The mother's body incloses the
daughter's body, imperfect and immature; and the daughter's
body at the same time incloses the still more imperfect and
immature body of the grand-daughter; so that we have three
generations mysteriously folded up together. It is necessary
to add here, that while these rapidly multiplying *aphides* are
females, they are not perfect females. The young broods are
not developed in a true ovarium, nor from perfect ova; but
the process seems to be one of internal gemmation in the
simplest sense of the word.

We have, however, examples of parthenogenesis amongst
Hymenoptera and *Lepidoptera*, in which perfect females, with

all the generative organs normally developed, prove prolific without any conjugal intercourse with males.

Dzierzon, a Catholic priest in Prussian Silesia, announced in 1845, that the eggs from which the male bees or drones originate are produced and developed by the sole inherent power of the mother bee, without the action of the male seed. In 1863 this doctrine of Dzierzon was fully confirmed by the microscopic investigations of Von Siebold and Lenkhart. The queen bee, as is well known, receives the embraces of the male only during the hymeneal flight. If her wings are crippled so that this flight cannot be taken, she lays eggs which produce only male bees. The workers again, with whom no nuptial rites are possible, sometimes lay eggs, and these always produce drones. It is a curious fact, that in the agamic reproduction of *Aphidida* the offspring is almost exclusively female; while in the agamic reproduction of *Aphidæ* the offspring consist entirely of males.

A still more curious illustration of agamic reproduction is presented by the *Psychidæ*, a family of butterflies. Here the female is in every way perfect, and endowed with seed-vessel and with copulating pouch. But no copulation is accomplished and no spermatozoa take part in the process of reproduction. The eggs, also, are perfect and with perfect micropyles, but they undergo development without any preliminary fertilization. Amongst these creatures, indeed, reproduction seems to be permanently agamic, without even the occasional occurence of gamogenesis. The search for the male insect has now been continued for many years, but no males have been found. In a word, these wonderful *Psychidæ* are all females and all virgins, with no fierce masculine mates to annoy them with conjugal importunities, and no tempests of sexual passion to disturb the serenity of their lives.

Many other examples of agamogenesis, including also many examples of true parthenogenesis, might be mentioned here. They are so numerous, indeed, that it would hardly be rash to assert that non-sexual reproduction is of quite as common occurrence in the animal kingdom as sexual reproduction; and

that one-half of the living creatures that are born into the
world are born without the instrumentality of male ancestors.
But the examples which I have given are sufficient for my
purpose,—are sufficient, that is to say, to sustain my assertion that in the process of reproduction sex is not a primitive
and fundamental factor, but that it is in reality only a secondary
and complemental factor. It is, indeed, in the reproduction
of the higher animals an indispensable factor, but it is not
primitive and fundamental inasmuch as its agency is not invoked at the beginning of the development of the new creature.

Contrariwise, the development of the new creature amongst
the higher animals is always commenced by the mother alone ;
is always commenced during the mother's fœtal and larval
life ; and is always in the beginning a process of gemmation
or segmentation,—an outgrowth of a portion of the mother's
own body. When the development has reached a certain
stage of progression,—a stage as high and as complex as can
be attained by the unaided action of the maternal forces, and
when without some additional energy the development would
be arrested and the effort to produce a new creature prove
abortive, then it is that the mysterious agency of sex is invoked, and that the masculine energy becomes a factor of the
advancing development. New conditions, both static and
dynamic, are incorporated into the developing ovum, a more
active evolution is established and a higher development becomes possible of accomplishment.

THE DEVELOPMENT OF THE OVUM.

Let us return now to the fertilized human ovum, and mark
the stages of evolution through which it passes, until it stands
before us a fully developed human creature. The transition
is surely astounding,—from a microscopic speck of homogeneous bioplasm to a man fearfully and wonderfully made.
The most daring imagination might very well be staggered in
the effort to grasp the tremendous conception.

And yet the agencies at work are of the simplest possible character. They are these four:

1. The enlargement of cells.
2. The segmentation of cells.
3. The arrangement of cells.
4. The differentiation of cells.

In their last analysis enlargement, segmentation, and differentiation, are resolved into modifications of growth ; so that the fundamental processes of organization might be reduced to two, namely, the growth of cells, and their arrangement.

If we had commenced with the unfertilized ovum, the first stage would have been that of the conjugation of cells. But this has been sufficiently considered already. We found that the germinal vesicle is a nucleated bioplast ; and that the spermatozoon is also a nucleated bioplast. But the fertilized ovum which is the product of their conjugation, is destitute of a nucleus,—is homogeneous and structureless. It finds its way into the uterine cavity, and attaches itself to the *membrana decidua*, by which it becomes invested just as did the original germ-cell in the ovarian stroma. But of these investments we have nothing to say. Our business is with the developing ovum.

The first metamorphosis which this exhibits is the metamorphosis of growth, enlargement, continuous development— the metamorphosis of addition.

The second metamorphosis which it exhibits is the metamorphosis of segmentation, of discontinuous development— the metamorphosis of division. The single mass of bioplasm of the fecundated ovum is separated into many masses of bioplasm. But still, for a time, there is no differentiation among them. As far as we are able to judge, the segments, or segmentation spheres as they are called, are all exactly alike. They are all composed of unmixed bioplasm, of germinal matter, and as yet there is no formed material—no signs of structure to be seen.

Let it be understood without further mention that the two metamorphic processes already described, the process of growth, and the process of segmentation, continue indefinitely, and we will turn our attention to the next stage of the evolution.

This next stage, the third, is a process of simple arrangement. It is metamorphic of the whole mass of the ovum, not of its separate segments. The segmentation-spheres march like soldiers to their appropriate places, and arrange themselves into three ranks—the three germinal plates, or blastodermic layers of the embryo. The first of these layers, the external layer, is called by Remak the sensational layer ; the second or middle layer, the motorial layer; the third or internal layer, the intestinal or glandular layer. The process of arrangement does not stop with the formation of these primitive blastodermic layers ; but other arrangements arise successively within the layers, secondary, tertiary, etc.—arrangements of continually increasing speciality and complexity, and out of these are developed the various tissues and organs of the completed organism. How these arrangements are accomplished, whether as the result of spontaneous impulse and the faculty of amœboid motion on the part of the bioplasts concerned ; whether under the influence of external incident forces ; or whether through the concurrent action of both of these classes of causes, we will not stop to inquire. The indications of the antecedent causes are vague and shadowy ; but the fact itself, of arrangement, is clear and demonstrable.

This brings us to the fourth and last of the metamorphic processes which are concerned in the development of the fœtus, namely, the metamorphosis of differentiation. The arrangement of the bioplasts into rudimentary organs is already in a certain sense, a process of differentiation ; it is differentiation of the mass of the developing ovum. But the differentiation now to be discussed, is the differentiation of the separate and individual bioplasts constituting that mass.

Biological analysis shows that the organism is composed of organs, these organs of tissues, and these tissues of histological elements. Now it is to be specially noted here, that every separate histological element—every muscle-fiber, every nerve-fiber, every epithelial cell, every constituent structural element of bone, of cartilage, of connective tissue, and of all the tissues, is the product of the differential metamorphosis of a separate and individual bioplast. And inasmuch as in a fully developed human organism there are many millions of structural anatomical elements, so, for the formation of these, many millions of living bioplasts must have suffered metamorphosis and differentiation.

The natural history of every histological element involves these three problems:

1. The derivation of the germinal bioplast, out of which it is developed.

2. The character of the transformation to which it is subjected.

3. The cause of the special transformation, which is in each case accomplished.

In the earlier stages of fœtal development, the germinal bioplasts which pass by differential metamorphosis into the elements of tissues, are the segmentation-spheres of the ovum. In the later stages of fœtal development, and during all the varying periods of life subsequent to birth, the original store of segmentation-spheres having been exhausted, the germinal bioplasts must be derived from some other source. But from what other source *can* they be derived? There is but one possible answer. They are derived from the blood in the shape of white blood-corpuscles.

I have already indicated, again and again, that the segmentation-spheres and the white blood-corpuscles are of the same nature,—are homologues and analogues of one another. But is there any genetic connection between them? Most assuredly there is. The white blood-corpuscles are the lineal descendants of the original undifferentiated segments of the ovum, the inheritors of their features, their faculties and their functions. The process of segmentation, commenced in the microscopic ovum, continues through the entire period of fœtal evolution, continues also through all the stages of infant and adult life, never ceases, indeed, until the organism which it has built up ceases to live.

Nature never abandons a process which she has once adopted. She may, indeed, under the influence of changing circumstances, modify it in many ingenious ways, and even to such an extent that its identity is difficult of recognition. She may also supplement it with secondary and auxiliary processes; and these, in the progress of development, may gradually increase in importance until the original process is overshadowed by them. Nevertheless it is true, that Nature never changes her mind, and never repudiates anything that she has once indorsed.

While, then, it may be true that white blood-corpuscles arise by other methods than by segmentation of pre-existing bioplasts, as has been suggested in the section of this paper which treats of the origin of leucocytes, it is still not to be doubted that many of them may claim hereditary descent, through perhaps a thousand intervening generations, from the aboriginal unique cell of the impregnated ovum.

DEVELOPMENT OF THE BLOOD-CORPUSCLES IN THE FŒTUS.

Very early in the history of the fœtus, bloodvessels begin to be developed; and at the same time the primary corpuscles of the blood make their appearance. It seems to be a general rule that this development commences in that part of the organism where the heart is ultimately to be found.

In certain definite spaces some of the bioplasmic masses,— the segmentation-spheres become fluid or semi-fluid; and the bioplasts enveloping these spaces are condensed into definite walls, the coats of the future vessels. In the meantime other segmentation-spheres inside of these walled spaces retain their cellular individuality. These are the primitive white corpuscles. Other white corpuscles proceed from these by proliferation. Others still, bud out from the soft bioplasm lining the vessels, from which they gradually separate and drop into the vascular cavities. As yet, however, there is no circulation. The vessels do not form a continuous system. But other vessels are formed, communications are opened up between them, at length a general anastomosis is established, and the circulation begins. Hence, as we have said, the white blood-corpuscles are the lineal descendants of the segmentation-spheres of the ovum, and endowed with the same essential characters and functions,—their permanent representatives through all the subsequent stages of the life of the organism.

The passage of the segmentation-spheres into the white blood-corpuscle can hardly be called a metamorphosis or a differentiation. The change which occurs is rather in the surroundings of the segmentation-corpuscles, than in the corpuscles themselves.

But all the other morphological elements of the organism are the products of differential metamorphosis,—are derived from segmentation-spheres, or from white blood-corpuscles, by the transformation already explained of some portion of their bioplasm into some of the varieties of formed material.

The first of these morphological products of differentiation to be mentioned is the red blood-corpuscle. It was for a long time the prevalent opinion among physiologists, that in the gradual ascent by progressive metamorphosis of the elements of the food into the substance of the tissues, the white corpuscle was first formed, that this passed into the red corpuscle, and that the red corpuscle then passing through a still higher transformation became incorporated into the substance of the tissues, and specially of the higher tissues, as the muscles and nerves. But for several years this doctrine has been falling into disrepute ; and in several recent works on physiology the supposed histogenetic functions of the red corpuscle, and its derivation from the white corpuscle are both denied.

After the red corpuscle has finished its career of vital activity, it may be that the materials of which it is composed, passing by liquefaction and disintegration into the blood-plasma, are then appropriated by parsimonious Nature, unwilling that anything should be wasted, to the nutrition of the blood and of the tissues. But it is certain that it cannot subserve any purpose of nutrition while it maintains its organic integrity. It is also certain that its primary and special function is not nutritive, but respiratory. As to its derivation it is certain, that in the fœtus it first appears as the offspring of the proliferating segmentation-spheres; and upon analogical grounds it would be reasonable to conclude that in later life it springs from the white blood-corpuscles which have succeeded to the functions of the segmentation-spheres. That this presumption is also warranted by facts, seems to be no longer doubtful since the observations of Von Recklinghausen and Golubew on the blood of the frog, in which they were able to detect the intermediate and transitional forms which bridge over the interval between the two types.

As the next example of differential metamorphosis let us see how a blood-bioplast passes into an epithelial cell. The transformation is sufficiently simple. The peripheral layers of the bioplast cease to grow, harden, and are gradually changed from living bioplasm into formed material,—from matter that is homogeneous to matter that exhibits structure. This process of transformation extends deeper and deeper into the bioplasm until we have a central nucleus of living bioplasm enveloped in a shell of formed material; and this is the type of the epithelial cell. A sufficient number of these agglutinated into a sheet-like expansion makes an epithelial membrane. The varieties of epithelium, as pavement-epithelium and columnar-epithelium, depend on the pressure and other incident influences to which the individual cells are subjected.

The muscle-fiber is formed essentially in the same way, by the metamorphosis of a bioplast. The structural material which results is of a different character, and assumes an elongated, spindle-shaped form. It has been suggested that during its formation the bioplast which is undergoing differentiation, moves forward leaving a string of formed material along the path it has travelled.

Cartilage is formed by a strictly analogous method; the only difference worthy of note being that fusion of the separate cells occurs in an earlier stage of the metamorphosis, and is so complete, forming a sort of plasmodium, that their special boundaries are entirely obscured. But each little mass of bioplasm still marks the central part of a constituent cell, and the so-called intercellular substance is formed material as before.

After the same general fashion are formed all the structural elements of the body, but it is not necessary to our purpose to pursue this part of the subject further.

In the development of every tissue there are two processes which must be carefully discriminated from one another, namely, the process by which the morphological elements of the tissue increase in size, and the process by which they increase in number. How the individual structural element increases in magnitude is easily understood,—how, for example, a muscle-fiber grows. But by what process is it that the number of fibers in a muscle is augmented, that a new muscle-fiber is added to those already in existence? This is a question not so readily answered. Does some growing muscle-fiber subdivide into two? Or is some new germ introduced from without which developes into a new muscle-fiber? The more we consider the problem, the more it is seen to be evident that if the division of a muscle-fiber is possible at all, it is only possible during its inchoate and, so to speak, larval condition. The fully developed muscle-fiber could be divided only by a process of considerable violence. And if the living bioplasm within the fiber were to undergo division the separated segments would remain imprisoned so that development would not be possible unless the enclosing walls were torn assunder to allow them exit. It is not easy to believe, then, that muscle-fibers originate in the proliferation of muscle fibers. And, inasmuch as the same reasoning is applicable to all the other structural elements of the tissues, it would seem to follow as a necessary generalization, that structural elements such as muscle-fibers, nerve-fibers, epithelial cells, and the like, are never derived directly from pre-existing structural elements of the same kind ; but rather that each must spring from a germinal bioplast, introduced from without, through the process of differential metamorphosis. We know that this is the rule in the earlier stages of fœtal development; and we have no proof that a different plan is adopted in infancy, or in youth, or in adult age.

This is not altogether a new doctrine. Dollinger announced, in 1828, that all the tissues were built out of blood-corpuscles, which had penetrated the walls of the bloodvessels and found their way into the interspaces of the tissue-elements. I have not seen Dollinger's book, and know nothing of the details of his scheme. Whatever these may have been, it seems to have exerted little or no influence on the development of physiology, and was very soon forgotten. The difficulties that must have opposed its reception at that time, have been dissipated by the discovery of the amœboid character, and migratory habits of the white blood-corpuscles.

It has, indeed, been recognized for a long time that such highly-organized tissue-elements as muscle-fibers and nerve-fibers, for example, do not themselves undergo physiological proliferation. Of late years the prevalent opinion as to histogenesis has been that of Virchow, namely, that all the other tissues are derived from the connective tissue,—that the germs of the structural elements of all the tissues, normal and abnormal, except perhaps the epithelial, are furnished by the connective tissue-corpuscles. But the connective tissue-corpuscles of Virchow are simply masses of living bioplasm which have not yet undergone differentiation into formed material, but which are themselves everywhere surrounded by the formed material constituting this tissue, so that even if the proliferation of these corpuscles really occurred the liberation of the segments would be attended with some difficulty. This difficulty surmounted, however, these liberated segments would be of the same character as the white blood-corpuscles, and in the last analysis the two theories would amount to very much the same thing.

This problem as to whether the bioplasm of the structural elements of the tissues undergoes proliferation, is one of very great importance both in physiology and in pathology, and must be examined a little more thoroughly. We have seen that, in some examples at least of inflammation, the first generation of pus-bioplasts are emigrants from the blood. But how about the subsequent generations of pus-bioplasts which present themselves during the subsequent stages of the inflammation? Are these also derived from the blood,—later colonies but of the same origin? Are some of them natural offspring of these adventurous emigrants, native as it were and to the manner born? And among these teeming myriads are there others still which have been derived by proliferation from the living bioplasm of the inflamed tissues themselves?

When the discovery was made of the facility with which blood-bioplasts pass through the walls of the vessels and the meshes of the softer tissues, and of the fact that vast numbers of bioplasts are engaged in these inflammatory migrations, there was a very general disposition indulged to consider all the bioplasts of pus to be emigrants from the blood.

But there is good reason to believe that bioplasts which have emigrated from the blood continue to undergo proliferation in their new habitats; and the origin of other bioplasts by proliferation of connective tissue-corpuscles, and by proliferation of inflamed epithelium has been so clearly demonstrated by thoroughly competent observers, as to be no longer doubtful. The rationale of these last processes is easily understood. In consequence of the inflammatory irritation there is an increased flow of nutritive material to the inflamed part, and an increased activity of nutritive appropriation on the part of the bioplasm of its structural elements. This bioplasm consequently grows rapidly, and instead of passing through its normal physiological transformation into formed material, undergoes rapid proliferation. The result is that the formed material which envelopes the bioplasm is rent into fragments and destroyed, while the newly formed bioplasts are set free to devour, to grow, to proliferate, and to wander without restraint, no longer conserving the natural functions of the organism, but quasi parasitic and destructive.

As a pathological phenomenon, then, we must admit the proliferation of the bioplasmic nuclei of the elements of the tissues. But it must be borne in mind that the proliferation extends only to the nuclear bioplasm, and not to the whole substance of the tissue-elements ; that it is a pathological and not a physiological process; and that the products of the process are not tissue-elements but pus-bioplasts. For the most part, as has been said, they are parasitic and destructive. Whether they ever become naturalized in the organism, and subservient to the purposes of life has not as yet been specially investigated.

A question which has occurred to many is this, how is it that the blood-bioplast can be developed into so many different varieties of tissue-elements? How can the same sort of seed produce so many different sorts of fruit? There is only one answer, namely, this : That the special development of the germinal bioplast is determined by the action of incident forces, by the nature and nutrition of the part in which it takes place,—that is to say, that the character of the fruit depends very much on the soil in which the seed is sown and the influence of surrounding conditions.

Here, also, out of the study of phenomena such as these, rises into view the great law of infection ; a law which has heretofore been recognized only as a law of pathology, but which, in accordance with the definition which has been given of pathology, as simply abnormal physiology, must manifest itself, also, as a law of physiology. In obedience to this law, a bioplastic germ developing among muscle-fibers becomes a muscle-fiber ; developing among nerve-fibers it becomes a nerve-fiber, and so on. We see a sort of mixed example of the influence of this law of infection by contact in the influence which is exerted when a few scales of epithelium have been engrafted on the granulating surface of an ulcer. By the mere contact of the transplanted cells the adjacent bioplasm is transformed into epithelium, which soon extends so as to cover the ulcerated surface.

EXPLANATORY NOTE.

Here, for the present, this paper must close. I am fully aware how incomplete and defective it is, and would gladly make it better if circumstances were more auspicious. It has been written hurriedly, in the midst of many pressing engagements, and, worst of all, with but scanty access to books and authorities.

Nevertheless, I am satisfied that the statements of facts will be found to accord very generally with the latest observations. For the scientific or speculative use which I have made of the facts, I am, of course, responsible. If my speculations are sometimes a little startling, I am not the less satisfied that in the main they will turn out to be the true interpretations of many recondite problems in physiology.

It may be that sometime the opportunity will be afforded me of returning to the subject; and of filling up several gaps which occur in the physiological sketch which I have attempted; and, what is still more needed, to discuss in a way more nearly commensurate with their importance, the pathological relations of the white blood-bioplast, which so far have only been incidentally touched upon.

April. 1874.